# OUTSIDERS

*Roberto Saviano*
*Carlo Lucarelli*
*Valeria Parrella*
*Piero Colaprico*
*Wu Ming*
*Simona Vinci*

# OUTSIDERS

## SIX ITALIAN STORIES

*With an Introduction by Ben Faccini*

Translated from the Italian by
Abigail Asher, Ben Faccini, Rebecca Servadio,
Mark Mahan, N.S. Thompson and Chenxin Jiang

MACLEHOSE PRESS
QUERCUS · LONDON

First published in the Italian language as *Sei fuori posto*
by Giulio Einaudi editore s.p.a., Turin, in 2010
First published in Great Britain in 2013 by

MacLehose Press
an imprint of Quercus
55 Baker Street
7th Floor, South Block
London W1U 8EW

# CONTENTS

# Introduction

THE STORIES IN THIS COLLECTION FIRST CAME TO THE attention of the Italian public as part of a wider series of twice-weekly supplements sold with the national daily, the *Corriere della Sera*. In 2010, the publishing house Einaudi brought six of the stories together in a single book under the title *Sei fuori posto*, and in so doing united some of the most interesting voices contemporary Italian literature has to offer.

The Italian title was a play on words, broadly translatable as "you're out of place", with the "you're" in Italian also inter-pretable as the number six – as in six stories or authors (perhaps even a subliminal reference to Luigi Pirandello's influential play, *Six Characters in Search of an Author*). The present English-language title of *Outsiders* does not recreate the same ambiguity between words and numbers, but it does capture the sense of displacement first intended, and explicitly highlights a common denominator.

Indeed, it is gradually revealed that the central figure in each story is out of step with his or her surroundings. These are protagonists who are prey to feelings of dislocation, people placed on a collision course with society's standards. Yet their role is not merely to be an outsider or a kink in the system. Their purpose is to prise open and dissect the fissures and tensions of the worlds they inhabit. So it is that Roberto Saviano employs his main character to shine a light on the impoverished region surrounding Naples, and reveal the impact, in that precarious world, of Italy's participation in wars in Lebanon, Bosnia, Kosovo, Iraq and Afghanistan. Piero Colaprico, thanks to his protagonist, breaks into the cycle of poverty, drug-dealing and run-down housing in 1980s Milan. Valeria Parrella uses her character to expose the dictates of the class system in southern Italy in the period following the Second World War. Wu Ming's heroes live correlating struggles across time, trying to find roles for themselves in tumultuous pre-independence America and the stresses of present-day Italy. Finally, Carlo Lucarelli asks his principal character to lay bare the face of oppression in Italian-occupied Eritrea.

Within these distinct contexts the authors' protagonists wage unsung war. Defeat and humiliation await them unless they fight their corner. No-one will recognize their modest ventures. They must operate in the shadows, without becoming overt pariahs or outright challengers. They are isolated, loners and misfits.

In Roberto Saviano's "The Opposite of Death", seventeen-year-old Maria is widowed even before she has had the chance to become a bride. In the author's words, Maria is the girl who tripped up before she reached the altar. The way she expresses her grief is closely judged by all around her, and how she voices her pain might trip her up again. She has to face her agony alone in her childhood bedroom, watched over by her collectable Barbie doll and her old cuddly toys, dressed in black like a caricature of a southern grandmother. Hers is a world of extremes where war veterans are unemployed youths and where widows are lonely children.

The Eritrean maid, Aster, in Carlo Lucarelli's "Ferengi" is similarly caught up in a maze of paradox, both witness and central pivot to the unfolding narrative. She operates behind closed shutters, taking refuge from the stifling heat, in the breeze and darkness of the desert night. She has to care for her bedridden colonial master and submit to the whims of his conniving daughter-in-law. Although she is only a lowly and friendless maid, she is the one who delivers death and triggers the downfall of the exploitative colonial family lording it over her people.

Grazia, the peasant girl in Valeria Parrella's tale, undertakes a redemptive and solitary journey to earn her place in Italian society, stealthily countering the ingrained prejudice of the husband she has been married to for appearances' sake. It is only after years of swallowing her damaged pride, and trying to win the affection of a daughter from her husband's first marriage, that she merits the right to give birth to a child of her own, a child who will speak Italian rather than dialect and carry a surname with greater distinction than hers. Such are the forces of destiny.

It is the question of destiny, and its effect on the poorest and most outcast segments of society, which occupies the police investigator, Binda, in Piero Colaprico's journey into the labyrinthine stairwells of Milan's social housing blocks. Silvio Silvestri, nicknamed Pallina, a sacked teacher battling with chronic depression, is found murdered. As suspicion points at various people, those who are ostracized by mainstream society and those who struggle to keep their heads above water, have to prove their innocence to the police.

For the outsider, heroism is certainly not where it might be expected. "American Parmesan", written by the collective of five writers known as Wu Ming, shows Adalberto Rizzo, an Italian cheese-maker, becoming Albert Rice and a hero of American history, but the man's attempts at creating the perfect conditions for Parmesan in East Coast America set him at odds with modern Italians bent on maintaining the supremacy of the Parmesan brand. Adalberto Rizzo once crossed the Atlantic with his Italian cows, drawn by Benjamin Franklin's desire to improve nascent American cuisine. Centuries later, the historian Bonvicini has to weave a path for justice, one that will please today's Italians and finally mean recognition for Rizzo as an outsider within the history of America's melting-pot identity.

There is one piece in the present collection which does not, at first, fit the fiction mould of the other stories. Simona Vinci's

essay on isolation and loneliness, however, lends critical meaning to the overall outsider theme. At times incisive analysis of
current trends, at times confessional in tone, Simona Vinci finds
a connective thread between the need to isolate oneself from
the world – as Wittgenstein did in Norway in 1913 – and the
deliberate and creative reclusion of writers such as Emily
Dickinson, Samuel Beckett and J.D. Salinger. Vinci places this
within a wider backdrop of modern-day isolation and single-
dom, associating the depopulation of villages in the Italian Alps
with a 2008 survey which found that nearly four million Italians
often, or all the time, suffer from loneliness.

Using Simona Vinci's essay as a prism, it is tempting to try
to see this collection as a portrait of contemporary Italy with
its loneliness and its political and socio-economic instabilities.
Indirect comments on present-day Italy certainly abound. In
Saviano's narrative, Maria's husband-to-be, Enzo, is killed in
Afghanistan because he was forced to enroll in the army, a
career imposed upon him when the local bank refused him
a loan. The squatters and inhabitants of the social housing in
Colaprico's story live hand-to-mouth in miserable apartments
where a new washing machine is a source of jealousy, or even
a motive for murder. Wu Ming's impecunious Bonvicini finds it
nearly impossible to combine his onerous working life with his
family duties. Contradictions that have often typified Italy can
be detected throughout, particularly tensions surrounding the
family and the attachment to land. Saviano shows Maria
needing her family to act as a barrier against the outside world.

In Parrella's tale, Grazia is incomplete until she can create a protective family unit. Yet we witness a family tearing itself apart in Lucarelli's "Ferengi", and Simona Vinci depicts the family structure as a place of potential loneliness. Similarly, land and regional identities are seen as a source of pride, but emigration in some form, within Italy and beyond, features in much of the collection.

The Italian peninsula, its people and culture are a vital refrain even though the stories span different ages and geographies. The tales crack open the multiplicity of Italian identities. We are left, as in "American Parmigiano", with the impression that traces of the protagonists will always survive, and with them traces of Italy, from nineteenth-century Africa to eighteenth-century New Jersey. But it would be reductive – indeed it would diminish the scope and impact of the panoply of outsider characters – to say that this collection is just about Italy. These pieces are, first and foremost, stories about the human condition with a distinctive Italian slant.

Simona Vinci poses the central questions at the heart of this collection. What does it mean to be out of place? Who are we in relation to others? How can those on the outside change the course of their lives despite the odds being stacked against them? Are we not all on the edge of others, on the verge of history, on the cusp of events beyond our control? If anything, *Outsiders* is about the turmoil of nonconformity and the need for dissent. Italy has always been fertile ground for both.

*Roberto Saviano*

THE OPPOSITE OF DEATH

I IMAGINE IT AS A PLACE COVERED WITH SAND, FULL OF mountains topped with snow. Sand and snow together. Although sand and snow don't mix — they never mingle in anyone's dreams. But I always imagine dust, sand, markets swept by the wind, the same wind we have on our beaches here. And in the distance, the snow on the mountain peaks. And then turbans, many beards. And those clothes that swallow you up, that seem even beautiful to me. Clothes you wear when you don't want to be seen, when you want to be nothing more than fabric. At times I would like to wear them here, when I feel everyone's eyes glued to my face. If I smile, I'm smiling too much and I've forgotten him already; and if my eyes are swollen with tears, they mutter that I should pull myself together, as crying won't bring him back; and if I show no emotion at all they're already passing judgement: "she's gone mad with grief." And I wish I could hide myself under those blue bells, inside those burqas.

*

9

Maria closes her eyes and tries to picture Afghanistan. She takes some images that have passed through her mind in all these days and she describes them to me. It is the first time she's doing this with a stranger. But maybe I'm the only one who feels that I'm a stranger; maybe she saw me in church during the funeral, or perhaps she recalls seeing me when I came to play football around these parts, or came to the gym posing as a boxer and pretending to vent my feelings by pounding the punchbag. She speaks to me of a land she's never seen, but it is as if she knows every image broadcast by the T.V., every picture that's appeared in the newspapers: it's as if she has trained her eye to catch every detail behind the shoulder of each journalist reporting from Kabul, or in the articles in the women's weeklies that are packed with photographs.

Afghanistan has become a land that she mentions every day, more than she mentions the name of her own town. It's always right in front of her. It's a strange name – hard to pronounce; in her dialect it's twisted into Affanìstan, Afgrànistan, Afgà. And around here the name is linked not with Bin Laden or the Taliban, but chiefly with Afghani hashish – the best kind there is, the kind that came through here in small bars like gold ingots and that filled the garages, and that was for years the true attraction for everyone in the local drug-dealing piazzas.

Maria is nearly obsessed with Afghanistan. It's not an obsession that she chose for herself. It's a neurosis that she was unlucky enough to discover inside herself. The people close to her avoid any words that could even remotely remind her of the sounds of the word "Afghanistan". As if a simple sound could suffice to revive her pain or remind her for a moment, afresh, of the origin of her pain: "Afghanistan", as if she could ever forget even for a moment. Maria notices these unnecessary kindnesses. At first she was annoyed, the same way you get annoyed by those men who obligingly open doors with too much consideration or who apologize when using words unsuited for feminine ears. That's just false good manners, which serve to showcase the tact and subtlety of the noble seducer rather than expressing consideration for the person on the receiving end.

Maria cannot forget. She can't not think about it. It wasn't very long ago, but not even for one afternoon can she keep from thinking about what happened, and where it happened, and wondering what could been done to avoid it. She wonders, which you should never do. They train you, here, to consider everything that happens as inevitable. It's not the ancient fatalism that means accepting everything with open arms and bended knees. The daily training in taking everything as it comes, here, leads towards an attitude that's even more invasive. If it happened, you must try to turn it to your advantage – and this attitude prevents you from understanding. Understanding how things work, how things can be avoided, and where things come from. It's like taking every day as the worst one possible, but understanding how to profit from each one. Just a wretched little advantage that can wring some benefit from Destiny's moment of distraction, from a brief pause as the landslide crashes down on you.

No-one around Maria was asking how and why it happened. Everything happens just because it must. You just endure, and squeeze whatever you can out of what you must endure. You get what you can from whatever hits you, but you can never decide what alms you're permitted to request from the misfortune: what you deserve and why you deserve it. And the anger and pain seem to be born from the point where you realize that you cannot find any benefit in it.

But Maria is sick with questions. She asks the soldiers who were in Kabul with Enzo, and who have been back here for a while now; she asks anyone who is back for just a short leave. She asks anyone coming back from the latest war. She asks questions that she manages to jam in amid the bouquet of heartfelt and thoughtful words that they offer her as the widow, as the bride who stumbled before she even reached the altar. In town, there are veterans from every war, from all the recent wars. Veterans from those recent wars that aren't called battles or conflicts anymore, but "missions". Peace missions. Around here, though, the relatives, the village kids, the girlfriends, and the brothers all call them only: "the latest war". The latest war tosses the previous wars further back into the past. The latest war had been Iraq, a few months ago; for a long time before that, the latest war was Bosnia. Now, the latest war for people around here is Afghanistan. But everyone from the town of Casavatore, and from all the way over to Villaricca, on the other hand, went to Nasiriyah; and for the people inland, Lebanon is now the latest war. The soldiers left for Lebanon only a few months ago, but they are not mentioned. There are no shootings, no protest marches, no live video link-ups with T.V. shows that save families the cost of a phone call, no wives going on camera to show that the rounded little belly he left at home has ballooned hugely. So the fictional place is constructed out of JPEGs sent by the soldiers from the front in e-mails that serve to empty out their cameras' memory cards, and to back up the pictures to display to their girls and to show their families where they are working, and how they're getting by.

Newspapers do not want photos of ordinary days spent on the front lines. Army patrols, babies being carried, guys sitting on tanks with legs dangling, sunglasses and machine guns. They're all too predictable, or simply a daily report on wars that mustn't seem too everyday for anyone. Video is wanted, but only if you shoot at people who are wounded, only if you curse the enemy, only if you violate the rules of engagement, or if some enemy pounces and you're filmed while they're gutting you.

When the little kids from around here go on to school in Naples, or when they follow their fathers' and mothers' deployments to various barracks and end up in school in Rome or Turin, they don't understand when the new class talks about "the latest war". They're thinking of the wars where their fathers were or where their brothers are now, and they rack their brains to remember if that war is really the latest one, and to figure out if this is really what's being asked. And then they say: "The latest war was in Kosovo, 1999, my father was there", or "the latest war was in Afghanistan." The rest of the class almost always bursts out laughing – smirking because nothing is easier to answer than "What was the latest war?" They're not asking you about the Triple Alliance, or the year when the Armistice was signed after the First World War. They're just asking about the latest war – the easiest thing there is. Only a fool could get that wrong.

For the kids from my neighbourhood, though, layers and layers of other wars stand between the latest war they know and the latest war they're taught about in school. The earliest remembered war doesn't have Nazi uniforms and liberators' helmets; it's Lebanon in 1982 and the "Italcon" or Italian Contingent. But this isn't historical memory – no-one reads a book to remember this; it's simply a bar-stool memory: stories you tell while cursing the bank for refusing to defer your mort-gage payments, or while unwrapping the new calendar that the army sends you each year.

If you say "veteran" and "the last war" elsewhere in Italy, you're flooded with images of grey-haired heroines of the anti-Fascist Resistance. But this place is full of veterans who are very young. Veterans who are raring to redeploy, veterans who come home and invest all their earnings in a bar. Or they open a restaurant with their comrades in arms – they start out by splashing out on marble countertops and chefs and then, almost always, things start going sour. And then they deploy again to the front somewhere, if they're still the right age, if they haven't taken a hasty discharge, if they've kept up the right contacts that can get them a posting. Civilian armed security guard teams all across Italy are full of veterans because – after you have escorted a food convoy and defended it from K.L.A. guerrillas or from Aidid's troops – you can escort a junior minister or a government witness without dreaming every night that you're getting blown up.

The majority of the troops on missions are soldiers from the South. More than half of the Italian war dead are from the South. This province is full of veterans. Soldiers who have returned from Bosnia, and from Mozambique before that; soldiers back from Kosovo, soldiers back from Somalia, soldiers back from Iraq, soldiers back from Lebanon or awaiting a return to Lebanon. Soldiers who sent back only their bodies, burned and lacerated and dismembered.

It's full of soldiers here. Paratroopers from the Folgore brigade, riflemen from the Garibaldi brigade, paratrooper carabinieri from the Tuscania regiment, as well as the Alpini mountain infantry, and the San Marco battalion, and the Sassari mechanized brigade. There's hardly anyone around here who hasn't thought of enlisting, at least once. Only if you were born without a kidney or with a club foot; only if you have retinitis pigmentosa that will blind you, then no: those are the only obstacles that keep people from yearning to join the army. And people apply anyway, even in those cases. People try; it's up to the military doctors to discover the problem. People hope for a moment of distraction – for a deaf and blind doctor. Around here, even one-legged guys would try to enlist. And although in the old days of conscription, thousands of young guys got themselves exempted because of fictitious anal fistulas, or paid a fortune for a cup of blood-contaminated urine as a sample that would ensure they would be ruled unfit, this no longer holds, now that "army" means a job and salary.

Where I come from, the place to register for enlistment is at the service counter of a barracks facing the Royal Palace of Caserta. They come in dozens of cars and, since it's a tourist spot, they park far away and then, carrying a thermos full of coffee, wrapping themselves in blankets, they line up at night to wait and be the first to deliver an application the next day. After the law abolishing the draft, the volunteers feel unlucky; they would have happily taken advantage of the loose rules from that era that would have counted them fit to serve. Conscientious objection was a choice for left-wing guys who could spend that whole year not earning anything – almost all of them were students. For others, however, it was a year of lost earnings, and the draft was an opportunity, a chance to test whether barracks and uniforms were better than the construction site and the tool shop, better than driving trucks halfway across Europe, or working behind a bar.

All of Maria's relatives have enlisted or tried to enlist, and Maria knows all the veterans' wives and girlfriends. Besides, not knowing these women would mean that she spent no time with her peers.

"They can't help it: they always ask me weird things, like

'How do you know if they've sent your husband to a dangerous place', or 'What do they tell you before letting you know about the death?' They want to protect themselves, to know so they won't be caught by surprise, to learn from a friend who has had misfortune – like a vaccination, to understand it immediately, or to try to avoid it. All my friends who have boyfriends off at war want me to tell my story. When I finish, they ask me to tell it again, and after that they ask me to tell it over again. 'Let it all out!' they say, but the truth is that they don't want to miss a single detail. And the more they listen to me and look at me, the more they fear ending up like me. So they try to understand everything, and I can already picture them going home and e-mailing their boyfriends to tell them to do the exact opposite of what Enzo did."

Maria appears to be wise beyond her years. She got it somewhere, from the distillation of identical moments she's living through, where the minutes seem to run on longer than the years she has lived, minutes colliding with each other, pressing together in this life of hers that no longer has the breadth it should have.

"These women don't understand that these things can't be decided by others. Where their boyfriends will go, what they'll do. They are commanded. And their own lives don't depend on them. But how can I explain that? They believe that listening to me will help them save their boyfriends – and why shouldn't I let them believe it?"

Maria's hands are sweaty, and she twists them together. We

decide to walk through the town; no-one is watching us. Or rather, everyone is used to always seeing Maria with someone by her side, as if it were an addition to the comfort of her family. She looks like a child, especially her feet. They're fitted with little shoes that I'm sure she bought in a children's shop – the size is too small, a size you can't find in shops for adults. And the style is doll-like, with four cut-out holes on the top of the foot. She wears her hair in layers, with two clips at the temples that keep it from falling in her eyes. Her nose is pointed, like a little blade stuck between her cheeks. She wears black tights, a big black sweater, and a black jacket. She has no make-up. There's something oriental about her eyes, perhaps because they are in such perfect harmony with her petite, almost porcelain, body. She already has a widow's mask. She seems like a miraculously youthful version of her grandmothers, of her mother. Some-times when she's dressed in dark clothes like this – and occasionally she even wears a black kerchief on her head – it's laughable: she looks as if she's pretending. Like a little girl in front of the mirror, with her feet swimming around inside her mother's shoes, with huge necklaces running from her skinny neck to her navel. That's what Maria seems like, a caricature of her grandmothers in their permanent mourning clothes. She and all the women in her family have been dressed in black for months now. Soon it will be a whole year. An everlasting mourning that does not end. The mourning for Enzo occasion-ally includes some other young man who drops dead, gets killed, passes on. And the guy generates mourning that extends to everyone: neighbours, friends, aunts, distant cousins. In my town, all my aunt's friends always dressed in black, because there was always a boy who had been killed; a distant relative falling from some scaffold; because respect always had to be shown for some family that had lost someone. And when there was nothing to mourn, they continued to wear black because soon, surely, there would be something. So you might as well never take it off. When someone in his sixties dies – someone old – when someone dies of illness, close relatives can be the only ones wearing mourning; but when a young man dies, then it must be everyone. Like a shared burden, or a misfortune from which there is no escape.

Where I come from, when someone dies in war, everyone in the apartment building dresses in black. As a child I would look forward to baptisms and to Christmas when I could see the women of my house dressed in something other than black. Baptisms meant that they had to wear another colour, and Christmas required red. But my aunt was embarrassed: she was so used to black that she wore dark colours anyway; she couldn't see herself in colours. Once I blurted out: "Black even at Christmas, dammit – who died?"

"No, no, can't you see? This is blue."

In Maria's house, too, all the women were in black.


Maria invites me in. Her room is just as I expected. Still the same as when she was little. Posters, oversized cuddly toys, even a display case with one of those super-luxury collectors' edition

Barbie dolls that parents prevented you from playing with – just for show. A room that she expected to leave behind when she moved to a house, as a married woman, but where she is now trapped as a widow. On the computer there's a small picture, the kind you buy in San Gregorio Armeno: the Gulf of Naples lit by small lights that represent the rush of lava. A small object that makes something beautiful out of the time-worn postcard-cliché iconography. Naples seems so far away from this town. I ask her about the computer. As I imagined, she bought it because of Enzo's departure for Afghanistan.

"We had one e-mail account, and no-one knew the password except for us two. Enzo was jealous: he was afraid that I'd write to someone I met in a chat room. But I downloaded the software to chat with him – with no-one but him."

Perhaps she's lying, but she's right to lie. All the girls around here bought computers when their boyfriends left. For e-mailing, and chatting when they were both online. Free or nearly free communication. Ever since the military bases got computer centres, the number of internet contracts and broad-band connections shot up around here. The local technician who installs the Fastweb routers is a veteran who was in Somalia; he learned how to use wires and screwdrivers in the Folgore brigade. And whenever he can, he always goes to the homes of soldiers' girlfriends first; he tries to prioritize their needs, as if a remnant of warrior's honour keeps him feeling as if he's a member of a community of fighters.

In Maria's room there are pictures of Enzo everywhere. Enzo at the beach. Enzo training in the gym. Enzo kissing her. There's a very sweet one that makes me laugh: Enzo holding her up in the air with both hands, horizontally, like a dumb-bell, the kind used by Olympic weightlifters. Enzo was not muscular. He had the athletic body of someone who will become a boxer, but a flyweight.

And then a picture with the Colosseum behind them. The classic tourist tour of Rome.

"Yes, that's just before he left for Afghanistan. The first time I went to Rome. We went to see the shops selling the most beautiful wedding favours, the least tacky ones, the ones that aren't used by everyone; and then at home in our town we were going to look for the ones most like the Roman ones."

Maria's friends, the ones who went to college, had said she would make a great impression if, instead of giving out wedding favours, she gave out lapel pins for Emergency, the N.G.O. for war victims. Emergency operated in Afghanistan, too, and who knows? – maybe somewhere in Kabul Enzo would meet that doctor with the white beard, Gino Strada.

"I really did consider that Emergency thing. But can you imagine all my relatives? They would not get it – that little bow, and that badge; they couldn't have put it on the shelf at home along with the wedding favours from all the other family weddings. They would have thought that my family couldn't even afford favours for their daughter's wedding."

Maria pauses frequently when she's talking about these

things. She must be careful not to lose herself. It is risky: often she gets lost chasing memories and cannot find the breath to speak, suffocating on everything that didn't happen. Like a fish pulled from the aquarium. Choked by oxygen.

She manages to tell me about that morning. She had returned home with the wedding favours, chosen on her own, but identical to the Roman ones she had seen with Enzo; she had not yet bought the dress, but she had already tried on three styles, and she had her eye on one in particular.

"My brother answered the phone; it was Enzo's mother; he called out to me. He was still on the phone with her when he told me that Enzo had been wounded, that the Taliban had attacked a truck, a tank with Enzo inside. But Enzo was not in any tanks or trucks; he had never sent me any photographs where he was close to the tanks.

"They told me right away, so I didn't get scared immediately. I had no saliva in my mouth, but my brother continued talking with Enzo's mother and so I thought that it wasn't serious. I figured that people tell you bad news slowly. That the carabinieri car would have gone to Enzo's mother's place, and then his father would have told my father, and my father would have called me in there, into the living room, where people bring you in to tell you terrible things, saying: 'I must talk to you, Maria,' and in the meantime I would have realized that something serious had happened. Instead, while I was just sorting out the wedding favours, my brother – still on the phone – mumbled the news to me. Who expected it? I couldn't get scared right away. We turned on the television, but there was nothing; we looked on the internet – nothing. We phoned the numbers we had, Enzo's friends, but no-one knew, nobody said anything. The first news I got from T.V.; then they called us and told us that Enzo had been in an armoured vehicle outside Kabul, and that his vehicle had driven over a landmine and the mine had exploded and the vehicle upended and that someone died, but that Enzo made it."

In fact, what blew up the armoured vehicle was not a simple anti-tank mine but a remote control; the Taliban had been waiting for an Italian convoy to pass before they triggered the bomb. In the armoured vehicle were four soldiers. It flipped right over. The soldiers' eardrums popped immediately, plunging them into silence. Enzo had no legs; the wounds were cauterized immediately; the femoral artery was closed off; and the armoured vehicle went up in flames. The fire went right out, as if to make him suffer even more: the vehicle suddenly became a furnace, and they had exploded eardrums, and metal plates like flying scimitars were cutting right through everything. The explosion sent one soldier against the roof of the vehicle, breaking his neck instantly; two others survived; Enzo's body was half in and half out.

The Taliban had blown up the convoy. The armoured car hadn't armoured anything. It was cut open from beneath, and splinters rained inside.

"We were told he could be saved, that's what they told us . . ."

In the village, people immediately began to make banners to welcome him home; the family couldn't leave the house without everyone asking – they all wanted to know about Enzo.

"Even the bank manager – the one who hadn't wanted to give us a loan because we couldn't give guarantees – even this guy, who was one of the reasons that Enzo had done the maths and had gone to war, he kept coming up to my mother and saying: 'A loan for the kids – count on me as soon as the caporale gets back; as soon as the caporale gets back, come to me!' I wanted to spit in his face, but a woman doesn't do such a thing."

When he landed in Rome from the Kabul flight, they took him to the hospital. The town almost celebrated; people had even bought fireworks, and the best pyrotechnicians in the area were ready to do a show for free. It felt festive. But there was no homecoming. Enzo died. Perhaps after the attack there was just one last breath in his lungs, just enough so the first bulletin could report that he was not dead; enough air that they could avoid breaking the news of too many front-line deaths. And they spread out the death reports, one at a time, one a week.

"I realized he was dead from how my mother approached me. She hugged me; it had been years since my mother had hugged me. She hugged me and started to run her fingers through my hair, because she knew there was always a lull before I reacted to something. In a short while I destroyed everything I saw, including the television – I threw the wedding favours off the balcony; I did not want anything to survive Enzo. Not even things. Not even me."

Maria insisted that she wanted to see him, she had to see him, she had a right to see him. But the bodies of the war dead could not be displayed. Even death has its grammar. The war dead cannot be studied by those who do not know war's ferocity. And Maria's family believed she could not approach a shattered body. Enzo was there, on a table in a military hospital in Rome. Like all the dead. In a room identical to other rooms in millions of hospitals, where they all end up, just like all other morgues, whiteness and tiles and the smell of disinfectant. There was little, too little of him. Enzo's brother had seen him, had identified him, but could not touch him: just one kiss on his forehead risked peeling off the skin that had remained stuck to the bone. Maria insisted. She wanted to see him, she wanted to be with him one last time. But she could not see him like this. So they made a pact, one of those pacts that you extort from people who are powerless – with their swollen eyes and filled with mucus from weeping – but who are firm in their intentions. Enzo's brother let her go into the morgue with her eyes covered. He had one hand in Maria's right hand and the other over her eyes. That other hand that could prevent Maria's curiosity from prying open her eyelids for even a moment. That's the way he brought her close to the table, close to Enzo.

"I don't know how he came back, I didn't see what they did to him. I smelled a terrible odour, like chicken skin when it's burned. But that was not his smell. I felt that he was there and

I felt him, beside me. I felt that something had been saved. It was as if I had entered a room that he was in."

Maria gripped Enzo's brother's hand so tightly that her nails, long and manicured like those of a woman about to get married, sank into his palm. But Enzo's brother said nothing about it, or he didn't feel it.

Enzo had enlisted in the army with the specific intention of being sent on missions. He had stopped going to the gym, where he was one of the best boxers. People believe that guys enlist for the money. And, too often, people use the word "mercenary". Mercenary. It sounds good, strong, fierce; it sounds crucial enough. It has an air of romantic inspiration. A fighter should fight not for the money but for love of country. What a joke. And guys from around here don't even take offence when they're arguing and the other guys their age insult them by calling them "mercenaries". It's hard to see why soldiers are the only ones who shouldn't consider the pay for their work. When they go on missions, their pay is tripled, sometimes even quadrupled. But then there's all the rest of it. The rest of it is the chance to grow, to do something that has the weight of respectability, of a commitment, of the annual bonus, of vacation time, of being valued as someone, a person to be considered. And the chance to see a bit of the world. And, for some, to see what it's like to make war, to shoot and get shot at. To invade, strike, challenge. But, for many, just going and getting back as soon as possible, all in one piece. And bringing some pictures home with them.

Soldiers from different wars. Southern Italy is the leader in violent deaths for young people. As she told me about her blind reunion, Maria's cheekbones were wet with tears. But she stopped crying almost immediately. As if she had decided to stem the tidal wave starting to rise.

The first time I saw her she was embracing a coffin, on her knees. In church. Small, she was smaller than she is in now, right in front of me. I feel like I'm seeing her again. To quell her memories, Maria gets some water and starts to drink. The water drips from the corners of her mouth. Everything about her seems silently hungry. Hunger, thirst, sleepiness. Everything seems to be a sign of life, a life that pulsates under her skin, but like a fuel that does not permit her to turn off, not even for a moment. Doesn't permit her to surrender. Maria makes a gesture – a lovely gesture – the kind you don't forget once you've seen it close up, and you can feel your blood flowing through you. It is a gesture that my mother always made when she felt hot. A gesture that people make in the country. They dip their fingers in the trace of water at the bottom of their drinking glass and then slide their fingers down their chest, right between the breasts, where the sweat doesn't run easily, like a quick rinse. The gesture must be instinctive, because it is just as insolent as picking your nose or removing a piece of meat stuck between your teeth. Yet it's done so naturally. At that moment I see the pendant that Maria is wearing. Not a cross, nor zealot's religious charm, nor a saint's portrait, nor holy rosary. But Enzo's dogtag. Deformed by the fire and the heat. And I'm reminded

of a scene from Enzo's funeral. All his boxing friends from the
gym had their hands bandaged, all of them in the front pews of
the church. When the time came for Communion, they didn't
line up in front of the priest; only the old ladies lined up, while
all the guys – military and non-military, veterans, fellow soldiers
– all took their dogtags in hand. Each one of them had a dogtag.
They scooped them from their chests and at the very instant
when the priest lifted the Host and offered it to the old ladies,
the guys put their own metal Host into their mouths. I looked
around. Everyone did it. I picked up my own dogtag and pressed
it between my teeth. I wear a dogtag and it feels like I've worn
it since birth. It is a military dogtag; it's got my first name,
surname, date and place of birth, blood type and a sentence
from Terence in Latin. Just enough to identify me, enough to
synthesize what I am: to carry myself in written form on my
own chest. Everyone or almost everyone I know has a dogtag,
a dangling metal biography. It's like a stylistic feature of youth
on the outskirts of cities, a provocation, a declaration of a
permanent state of metropolitan conflict. As if there's a need to
feel like soldiers at all times, even without an army, hating war
and loving combat. Actually, the dogtag is a key factor in understanding my land, my country, my people. One of my classmates
from lower secondary school, Salvatore, was identified thanks
to his dogtag.

Salvatore worked as an "escort", to help trucks brim-
ming unbelievably with drugs to avoid checkpoints. The trucks
stuffed with cocaine or hashish almost always travel with two

decoy cars that monitor the roads they'll take, alerting them to roadblocks or the presence of police cars and carabinieri. If there is a roadblock, the driver decides to leave the highway for several kilometres, and if that's impossible, a car comes into play that's called "the Wreck" in some neighbourhoods: a beat-up car that accompanies important shipments, always keeping a slight distance, and when needed it approaches the checkpoints with conspicuously dangerous driving so it gets stopped, permitting the shipment to pass undisturbed. Salvatore was a "Wreck" driver. He became famous because when he was escorting a truck and couldn't get himself stopped at the checkpoint, he didn't consider his mission a failure; instead he would rear-end a random car on purpose, deliberately causing an accident, so that the emergency would dissolve the roadblock and send the police cars to the disaster. Things ended badly for Salvatore. He went off the road after purposely slamming into a jeep. His car caught fire, but not completely, and so the flames enveloped him slowly; the motor burned and black smoke filled the car. When the firefighters arrived, Salvatore was completely burned. But they could immediately identify him because he wore a dogtag. He wore one, like everyone else. Name, surname, date and place of birth, and blood group. And on the back, his girl-friend's name. An addition to his metal biography.

Now doctors, firemen and policemen always reach for the chest, feeling around with their hands for a dogtag – to avoid checking pockets, pulling out I.D. cards, or asking the dying, "What's your name?" And when they don't find a dogtag, it is as if they're dealing with a novice, like some youngster who didn't put on a helmet, or the imprudence of someone who wanders unprepared through a war zone. The dogtag is a drag – it's uncomfortable. Every time you hug someone in the cold, this little postage stamp gives off a shock if it touches the other person's skin, and in the summer it gets glued down to your chest with sweat, and when you make love it dangles against the girl's nose or even drops into her mouth. Every one of my friends has shown off the bite marks that they claim their women have put onto their dogtags; I always squinted at the metal and never saw anything but microscopic scratches. Every scratch comes from a different female canine tooth, according to their tales.

A dogtag is a trace. The trace of a country at war. Of part of a country at war. A country at war that doesn't know it's at war. Of men burning on different fronts. Burning like Salvatore or like Enzo.

While we're talking and I'm trying to soften the embarrassment by showing her my dogtag, Maria leaps up and grabs a colourful dress out of the closet. She shows it to me. And amid all the dimness of clothes and shadow, it shines at me like a flashlight pointed straight at my eyes. We're three days away from her birthday. The dress that Maria will wear to her party is what she was planning to wear on the day she did her wedding paperwork. I realize I don't know her age. I've always taken it for granted that she was generically young. I ask: "How old are you?"

Maria looks at me, swallows. Perhaps no-one asks her this question anymore, in recent months: "Seventeen; eighteen in three days."

I think I've misheard her.

"Seventeen."

Enzo was twenty-one. Soldiers almost never have a specific age. When they are not considered killers, or ferocious, they're all generically young. But when their youth is cut short with a death notice, dying at twenty-one is too young even for a volunteer soldier who went to Afghanistan to pay for his wedding and the down payment on a house. And when you say the age out loud, the distance – from the event, from the uniform, from the duty, from the distant land – collapses and slams you right on the nose. That "seventeen", said so simply, the way people state their age, hit me like a glass door that you walk right into because it's so transparent. I had thought she looked like a child, and she was a child. She is a child. A child widow. A bride in white. Seventeen years old. It feels as if I'm gazing at something sacred. A kind of archetypal recurring image, a tragic Vestal from some historical period. The young girls widowed by young boy soldiers. Girls who became completely untouchable because they were always guarded by the spectres of their pro-spective husbands. That's what I looked upon. It tempts you to mouth the usual secular platitudes you overhear on the bus, that you hear on the political talk shows: that everything stays the same, that nothing changes, that there's no difference between past and present. But Maria herself blocks that temptation.

We go back out, and she brings me to the bar downstairs. It is full of veterans. It was started by a former paratrooper from the Folgore brigade. He had been in Somalia and then he got embroiled in his stories of photographs and turtles set under tank treads, and he took off, leaving the bar to his wife. Tommaso is there, glued to the video poker machine. He was in the war in Bosnia and he hates soldiers from any other mission. He spends a fortune on poker. He loses everything there is to lose on it. And he wins just often enough to motivate him to keep playing. Maria wants me to talk to him, or at least meet him. Tommaso is one of the angriest veterans, one who has had no peace since he returned.

"Nowadays the guys' camps are like Club Med; when we went, we shat ice in open fields; we had no satellite link-ups; when we wrote to our families we had to send postcards. Now they have gyms and internet, and they're never let out of the barracks. What do they know about Sarajevo, about Bulevar Selimovica Mese – what was called 'Sniper Alley'? They would have shit their pants. What do they know about M.R.U.D.s or PROM-1 mines? They know nothing about that. Nowadays they go just to parade around; we were really at war."

Tommaso hates other veterans, the ones who weren't in Bosnia like him. He always comes to stir up trouble with soldiers just returning from some mission; he hates the Iraq veterans most of all, because they have Nasiriyah, the symbol of that massacre, the memory of that sacrifice. And he wants his soldiers to be remembered, as if all the other massacres were

minor compared to his. Tommaso has troubled dreams; Maria
would like to help, but Tommaso is not approachable. They say
he keeps dreaming about the house-to-house patrol in Sarajevo
where watches with gold bands were dangling from dresser
drawers. As soon as the drawer was opened and the watch lifted
out, everything blew up. It was a trap: the drawer was connected
directly to a mine. A young guy got blown up right in front of
him. A young guy he had ordered to go and fetch the watch.
But these are just stories that people tell about him. He speaks
to no-one about his dreams. The only obvious thing about
Tommaso is his terror about his health – he's a hypochondriac.
He's just waiting his turn, but he's sure that sooner or later it will
come. Tommaso is terrified that he might father deformed children, sick from his contact with depleted uranium. So terrified
that he doesn't want children; so terrified that his wife has filed
for divorce. Maria provokes him to get him to fly into a rage; she
wants me to see the pain on Tommaso's face.

"So many are dead . . ."

"Worse than death. I've counted fifty-eight cases so far;
twenty-four dead from thyroid cancer, twenty-one dead with
their balls rotten and thirteen dead from Hodgkin's lymphoma.
I wish my memory didn't work so well. How many dead then?
More in Nasiriyah? – or more in Bosnia and Kosovo?"

Tommaso was Enzo's friend, but Maria discovered this only
a few days ago.

"It's strange, I realize that I know so little about Enzo. I
haven't got anything left because they didn't give us enough

time to make memories; they didn't give us enough time to have a past. We had only what happened, and nothing more. Once they took him away, they took everything from me. Someone should have told me that that's how it worked. That I had nothing yet . . . but I was getting ready to have something. And just when I was having it, I no longer had it."

Maria is left with wedding announcements and packets of invitations; she's left with whole parts of life that were designed and laid out, but that never became real.

"Of all the years we spent together, I have so little left; I know that he liked orange juice in the morning; that when he went to pick peaches at Villa Literno he would come home with a stomach ache because he would eat pounds of them. I know he loved Pietro Aurino, the boxer from Torre Annunziata; whenever Aurino had a match, Enzo would hitch a ride from the truckers who were his father's friends, to go and see it. I know that he liked to sleep with me, and that he wanted to leave this town, but here we could buy a house and all our people were here. I know that he was embarrassed to kiss me in front of his family. I know that I liked it when he scolded me out of his absurd jealousy, because if too many guys looked at me it meant that I was dressed in the wrong way. I know about the photos he sent me from Kabul, I know he liked the markets, he used to say that the locals didn't seem aggressive at all; he wrote that he wanted to take me to Afghanistan someday, and that everyone in Kabul was tired of war, and that everyone just wished for peace, like them. He wrote that he never expected the country to be so beautiful that it almost made you want to live there and to curse whoever had destroyed it. I know that he photographed the mountains for me. He said that when he was totally fed up, he could find silence wherever he needed it. Which he could never do at home. But there are many things I still don't know, that I still haven't found, that I have yet to discover, to understand, to learn about him."

She still doesn't know. It's as if Enzo continues on, as if he's not finished. As if there's still time. Maria is convinced that he continues on, that it's still possible to make what Enzo was continue.

"Do you remember Carmela?" she asks, and hard I as I try, I can't recall any girl with that name. Then it becomes clear. "If love is the opposite of death" are words from Sergio Bruni's "Carmela", one of the most beautiful songs ever written. The lyrics by the old singer from Villaricca trounce hundreds of verses by the greatest poets. Maria is certain. She can keep him from death – tear him away from death. She can do it, if she continues to love him enough. Like a reverse Eurydice who can hope to bring Orpheus out from the perimeter of Hades only if she doesn't take her eyes off him. A Eurydice who cannot get sidetracked, who doesn't want to take her eyes off Orpheus for even a moment.

Saying the word "love" is embarrassing. The tongue halts, as if it's tired of travelling a worn path, a path too often travelled, that it no longer wants to take. It's like a sound that is too well known. Like the phrases people chant without regard to meaning. Or like prayers that possess a sacredness that loses all content, with only the ritual remaining. There is a moment, however, when a word that's been slobbered by too many mouths, manipulated and distended by too many careless hands, becomes immaculate. There's no understanding why; one cannot backtrack and do it again. It just happens.

Hearing Maria whispering those lyrics, I felt I understood everything at last, as if she had taught me the most valuable of lessons, a lesson for which I had searched so far – down at the bottom of the barrel of words, in the metaphysics of theorems – while I actually had it right here, simple and solved. Pawing through a basket of thoughts and aphorisms, I had found unsatisfactory answers that did nothing to help me understand. And now every time I have no knowledge, every time I lack a definition, every time I fail to grasp a conclusive meaning – now I know the truth of love. It's the only truth that is still heard and understood in your very chest: the opposite of death.

TRANSLATED BY ABIGAIL ASHER

*Carlo Lucarelli*

FERENGI

*A dark tale in three photographs
and a drawing*

ABOVE ALL, THERE ARE THE NIGHTMARES.

Aster hears them coming because they are announced by a sound, like the lull before a storm, a hanging quietness which fills the ears and grates on the nerves, in anticipation of the noise that always follows.

The noise is a snarled wail, like the meowing of a cat. Aster knows it well and it no longer frightens her, even though the first few times it made her shake with terror, and she didn't want to look after the *ferengi* at night. Then she got used to the way the old man gasped in his sleep, the way his breath scraped and snagged between his teeth as if refusing to come out, and then how, all of a sudden, he would stop breathing and his mouth would open, as if frozen in the dark – and then the wail would come.

Aster has no idea what the old man dreams about, but she knows that all she has to do is get up from her mat and touch him and he stops. At first, as well as frightening her, it disgusted her, his pale naked body, the white hairs shining in the half-light, the sodden sheets wrapped around him, but she only had to touch him, lift his head, straighten out his legs, and he would stop. The old man would then go back to sleep and Aster would return to her mat, her head resting in the hollow of her arm, and she too would sleep until the next nightmare came.

Apart from filling her with fear, and repulsion of course, Aster also hated the old and ailing *ferengi*. The rest of the girls in the house carried out other tasks, some of them more strenuous, and the signora thought she had done Aster a favour by entrusting the old man to her.

"*Abbo*," my father, "*abbo*," the signora had said, "the barone, very ill, *homum*, ill, you understand? But he's *zubbu*, good, very good." He wasn't though. He wasn't "*zubbu*" at all, that old *ferengi*. In fact, he was bad. He stared at Aster with the only eye he managed to keep open, because the eyelids of the other were almost closed, as if they had been sewn together, and he followed her with his stare, grunting between his lips. And when she got near him, he hit her with his bony hand, as heavy as a claw, and it hurt her.

Aster had never understood why he did it. She was the one who cleaned, washed and fed him, the one who gave him enough to drink. She was the one who fanned his face when it was too hot, and the only one to cover his legs when a storm loaded the air with dampness. But still he hit her, tried to grab and scratch her. And Aster envied Saba who squatted down every day by the veranda tables to brush away the red dust from the road, and she envied Asmareth's trips to Massawa and back to fetch water from the ice house, and her sweat-drenched walks to Gherar to buy salt.

"The barone is a bit *obud*," the signora had said, touching her temple with the end of a finger, then she had shrugged and left Aster there, shut up in that big room, the walls covered with stuffed animal heads, skins, spears, masks and shields.

"The barone."

But Aster never called him that. For her, he was *zohoi*, the hyena, *tefenfani*, the disgusting one, but only in her thoughts, of course, never aloud. Then, little by little, he had become *areghid obud*, the old madman, then *areghid ferengi* and then just *ferengi*, the white foreigner.

And now that Aster is aware of what the *ferengi* wants from her, and she knows why he hits her and treats her badly, she can see that open eye of his and understand the whistling of his breathing as if he were talking. That is why she no longer knows what to call him.

## First Photograph

There is no first photograph. It would have been an albumen silver print, Victoria size, 126 × 80, mounted on a card with corrugated edges, but it has disappeared and all that is left is the plate and the photographer himself has no idea where he put it.

The photograph did not vanish because it got lost. It no longer exists because it was ripped into pieces and burned.

Officially, at least that is what they say, because it was taken on
the 29th July, 1900. The Caraffa brothers had struck a pose to
celebrate the opening of their new trading office in Asmara.
They had forced themselves to smile, in a way that was inappropriate for such a fateful day, because that very evening in
the Italian motherland, in Monza, the wretched hand of the
anarchist, Bresci, had taken aim and shot His Majesty King
Umberto I with three bullets to the heart (some say four). So
they got rid of the photograph and met with the approval of all
those who commented on its disappearance from the office wall
in Massawa.

But that was not the real motive for getting rid of the
photograph. And whoever had lived in the colony of Eritrea in
those last years and seen the albumen glass plate, and maybe
even tried to blow the dust off it to reveal its imprinted image,
would have understood.

The framing of the subjects is slightly out of focus. It is not
the fault of the photographer, it was the brothers who wanted
to have the writing on the door in the background: TRADING
COMPANY/BARONE CARAFFA AND BROS.

Looking at the photograph, the first of the two brothers,
Mauro, the taller one, is standing on the left. Stiff, his thumbs
tucked under the edges of his waistcoat up near his armpits, he
has always been the more serious of the two brothers and,
indeed, this time he is not really smiling. His lips are spread out
over his teeth in a static grin that looks as though it could last
for ever.

The other brother, Giovanni, has his hands in his front trouser pockets. He too is wearing a waistcoat and his pencil moustache is stretched above his lips in the same contrived smile. If they had been down in Massawa at that time of day and in that season they would not have been able to dress like that, not even for the duration of a photograph. In fact, Giovanni is thinking of settling permanently in Asmara. All the more so now that the borders are secure, and if colonial expansion got underway again it would be directed up at the plateau. But there are no signs of a major renewal of the Italian colonial effort. Asmara is little more than a village and, apart from the trading headquarters which have only just been built, there are few stone buildings. Moreover, Mauro cannot breathe at this altitude. He feels as if the rarefied air will disintegrate in his throat.

Even further to the right is another man. He is tall too, a little bent, with a pointy profile and curly hair: Vittorio Cappa has followed them up there to escape the unbearable heat of Massawa. He is smiling a lot, but only because he is drunk on *areki*, downed straight, without adding water.

And it is for this reason, because he drinks too much, that this top colonial civil servant, Vittorio Cappa, was nabbed falsifying accounts for the merchandise arriving in the colony. Signor Cappa had been a bit of a magician before he ended up like this. In his glory days no-one would have found him out.

Vittorio Cappa is no longer around. He disappeared shortly

before the carabinieri came to fetch him at his office, clacking together their handcuffs and chains as they went. And who knows where he is now? Perhaps he is back in Italy, or he escaped to the desert and is dead, or perhaps he went to Djibouti to set sail for some other place.

The problem is that a lot of the merchandise spirited away by Signor Cappa then reappeared in the trading offices of Barone Caraffa and Bros. That is why, when Signor Cappa vanished into thin air, they also got rid of all the ledgers which documented their activities together, and the photograph with it. They could not take any risks, of course, considering what they were up to.

## Second Photograph

The second photograph does exist, however; even if it is crumpled from being stuffed in the pocket of a desert jacket during the rainy season. It is an albumen silver print, Pocket size, 75 × 37. If there were smells in photographs, one would be able to understand why Barone Caraffa has his nostrils open so wide and why his neck is so straight, like a horse at full gallop. Everyone always thought it was his character, like that of a horse in a never-ending race, thin not because he did not eat, and sober not because he did not drink, but because he burned everything up, and fast.

The air the barone can smell is spiced with *berbere*, a mix of herbs and spices with no trace of pepper. The aromas are of cloves and ginger which widen his nostrils, overwhelming him, making his mouth water. Behind him, on a road in the background, an old woman covered in a white cloth is kneeling in front of a fire. She seems to be cooking something. The barone cannot see her. He has his back turned to her, one arm leaning on a little wooden table and the other lifting a glass towards the photographer, who took the picture while he was moving. And, in fact, the raised toast appears as one long white streak, like a comet.

A man next to the barone, a Frenchman, is making the same gesture, one arm on the table and the other holding a glass in the air. The hand around the glass conceals its contents. It is not *ciai* from the teapot, but rather white *zibibe* from a small flask which the Frenchman keeps in his pocket, hidden away because they are near to one of the city's three hundred mosques. The Frenchman still seems like a boy, even if he is not much to look at, thin and tense like the barone, and ill too. A grimace is distorting one corner of his mouth, and he cannot wait to put the glass on the table to scratch his bad leg with his hand. He has been told that he should return to Paris for treatment, because he could die from the pain in his leg, but he does not want to. He has too much business down here in this part of Africa, and too many rivals like the barone. The toast they're both making is, in fact, in the barone's honour; he has managed to sell more guns to Menelik, a lot of them, and modern ones too. The Frenchman's guns seem obsolete compared to the barone's Remingtons: he practically had to give them away.

"The guns you're selling will be used against the Italians," the Frenchman told the barone.

"Why? Menelik is a friend of Italy."

"He's weak at the moment, but when he becomes Negus of all of Ethiopia he may no longer be."

"We'll think about that when the time comes. I'm no politician, I'm just a trader, like you. Let's see."

"You're always the same, you Italians," the Frenchman had said, and then, as he was a poet, he quoted a verse which the barone did not understand. In any case he was already thinking of something else.

The barone was thinking of when he had arrived from Italy, stepping ashore in Massawa with Generale Saletta and the first Italians, and how he had rushed to get a message home, not to his sons, who were still boys, but to his trading partners who had been decorated for services to the state, and whom he would buy out two years later: the first, a *commendatore*, by beating him at cards, and the other, a *cavaliere*, by sending him to prison with the (not altogether true) accusation of embezzlement.

"Buy wood and stones for building", the barone had written in his message, "and buy as much as you can", because he had noticed on that rugged beach burned by the sun that there were only stumpy and contorted acacia trees, like fingers deformed by arthritis, barely good enough for fencing in goats, and no rocks to make walls and fortifications. The colony lacked everything – fabric, leather, iron, wheat, wine – and the business was potentially worth millions. And the barone urged his partners to buy for themselves, not for Italy. So they bought, and they bought in huge quantities; the generale, the barone's cousin and undersecretary at the ministry, was going to make sure they were awarded the contract for supplies.

If the second photograph had had colours as well as smells, it would have been much more beautiful, even faded by the rain. You would have been able to see the luminous yellow of the shutters, the blue of the inn wall, the bright green of the doors and the glowing red of the girl's dress on the threshold. She is the Frenchman's lover and he takes her everywhere.

The barone finds his young African girls wherever he goes. That is how he got the syphilis which nailed him to the sodden sheets of his bed.

But you cannot see this in the photograph. It was taken almost ten years earlier. The barone was still strong then, and lean, with sparkling eyes and a devil's little beard, happy to have ripped off his French poet friend who had written across one corner of the photograph, partly in French and partly in Italian, "*Harrar*, 3rd March, 1887, *à mon ami le baron*, you old bastard, Arthur Rimbaud."

More than the nightmares, though, it was *bereket*, the third coffee. It was then that Aster understood, and the memory of the expression she saw in the barone's eye disturbs her more than his nightly howling. Aster is good at making coffee. That is why they got her to do the least taxing jobs, first in the kitchen, then with the old *ferengi*, even though she has broader shoulders and stronger arms than Saba and Asmareth. "A pretty, strapping girl," Signora Ada says.

Now Aster no longer makes the coffee as often, only when the doctor comes. Then she helps with the injection by holding the barone down on his bed, her hands on his shoulders. The old man doesn't like it, but Aster is strong and she knows how to restrain him if he moves. As soon as the barone is calmer – and a sort of thin veil covers his eye, the way it does when old people quieten and seem to look into the distance – Aster dresses him. She pulls on his trousers over his thin legs. She fastens the desert jacket at his sweating chest. And she has even learned how to knot his tie, "in the republican way", as the signora says. Then Aster puts him in his wheelchair all on her own, because the old *ferengi* doesn't weigh a thing and she sets on his head a hat, rim tipped at an angle, the way he used to wear it.

That day it was raining outside, and Aster did what she had always done. The *ferengi* were sitting on chairs and stools under the porch, while everywhere around them the black downpour of the storm closed off the veranda like a wall. Beside her were Signora Ada, Signor Giovanni and Signorino Mauro, the doctor, the capitano, as well as others from Italy, and the barone in his wheelchair, a wise and faraway smile on his lips.

Aster crouches on the wooden veranda in the middle of the circle of *ferengi*, her dress raised up over her knees, her bare feet, one crossed over the other, tucked under her rear.

Aster toasts the coffee beans on the fire, tossing them in the long-handled pan. She watches them darken, taking out the bad ones and putting the others into a mortar. She grinds them until they become a powder which she pours into the long beak of the *jemena* together with the water, and when she feels it boiling on the red coals of the oven, she takes off the horsehair lid and pours the coffee into the cups.

"Can I have some more?" asked a *ferengi* who had just arrived from Italy, and whom everyone treated with the utmost respect.

"But of course," the signora said, raising her voice to make herself heard over the pummelling of the rain, "you have to turn the coffee at least three times, otherwise it brings bad luck; one should even do it five times."

"Oh goodness."

The third turn is *bereket*, the one that brings good luck. Aster knows it and this time, as she toasts the beans, she leans forward on her knees and blows the thick coffee smoke towards the guests, letting them inhale it more deeply than before.

It was then that Aster caught the barone's gaze. It emerged from the mist like the sun in a storm, and at that moment, in fact, the storm stopped. His vacant expression had gone, and there was no more wisdom left, just something ugly which hurt her.

The old *ferengi* had flared his equine nostrils, breathing in the smoke with a loud sucking noise. And he looked at her.

*Tzeloi*, *quora*, *tesfa-queretze*, hate, rage, desperation, Aster would have thought if she had known those words, and if she had been able to read his mind. And if she had been able to look through the old *ferengi*'s eyes into his heart, too, she would have seen his whole life, full of business, sex, *zibibe* and coffee, and him then crippled in a putrefying bed, as if in hospital, overwhelmed by nightmares.

But it does not matter because Aster understood these things anyway, as if she had seen them herself.

The barone started to growl and she almost knocked over the stove in order to catch him before he fell out of the wheelchair.

"Take him away!" the signora said. "Sorry, your honour, it's arthritis, and with this rain . . ." and then she added, "You'll see that afterwards he'll sign the agreement, I'm on the case, as always," – because the signora is reliable in this way. Aster has seen her many times, hunched over the small table, copying the barone's signature in exactly the right way, with the same swirls and flourishes.

It was then, as Aster was putting him back to bed and stroking his head as she did after the nightmares, that she understood that she did not hate the barone, that he was no longer a *zohoi*, a *fefenfani*, but only an *areghid obud*, and she took pity on him.

But it was just then, too, as he beat her on the back with his bony fist, and she watched as he hit her over and over again, that she finally understood what the old *ferengi* wanted from her.

## Third Photograph

If photographs had sounds as well as smells, it would be easier to interpret them. The third photograph is an Ambrotype 165 × 11, Album size, and also coloured in bright tones that have faded with time into pastel shades.

Even so, much can be understood from the positioning and the expressions. Signora Ada, for instance, is leaning towards Capitano Martelli, and her husband, Giovanni, is a little further away, on the left as one looks at the photo, almost out of the frame, his back slightly bent. Signora Ada's brother-in-law, however, the other brother, is not easily visible. Yet with the aid of a magnifying glass he can be seen in the big window of the Hotel Torino in the background, its facade of spires like an exotic theatre set. And Signorino Mauro is so tall that even though he is sitting at a table his head still sticks out.

Signora Ada is dressed like a Bedouin, or rather the way she thinks Bedouin women dress because she has never seen one. She is wearing a striped caftan and a pair of embroidered slippers with curled-up toes. She has an umbrella on her shoulder which she twists round like a yellow sun, until the photographer asks her to stop, please. She is playing with a necklace of black pebbles, and she wraps it round one finger as if it were a lock of hair, and on her hard mouth there is the kind of smile a servant girl might have when meeting a soldier on leave in the park.

Capitano Martelli is twiddling one end of his moustache

with the tip of a finger. His other hand is in his pocket, in that slouching pose Signora Ada liked so much the first time she saw him. He was prancing about on a dromedary in front of Forte Taulud, covered in dust, exhausted and heroic, at the head of a company of African foot soldiers. From that time on, the capitano has puffed his chest out a little further, to show off the medal he won at Adwa. The inscription on the medal reads that he earned the honour by fearlessly leading the retreat of a mixed group of alpine soldiers, infantrymen and members of the rifle regiment. But it was only because – from the Rebbi Areni hill to the village of Addi Cahie, where they were picked up by the local Askari cavalrymen of the Cheren battalion – the capitano was running so fast that he ended up ahead of the others. His orderly knew the truth. He had remained on the hilltop to fight with the few men he had left, until they were killed, one by one, and he was captured by a platoon of Galla horsemen. He would have denounced the capitano had it not been for the fact that he had caught typhoid in a village on the Amba mountain, where he had been a prisoner, and he needed money to return to Italy for treatment.

The signora and Capitano Martelli are lovers. No sounds are needed to understand that. The photographer knows it, too. As he was taking the picture he saw that Signor Giovanni was a little too far away, and he was about to tell him to get closer to his wife when he noticed his shoulders were too rigid, as well as his neck and jaw, and that he was deliberately turning away so as not to see, feigning indifference. Giovanni knew he was a cuckold, or a "*coinnuto*" as the photographer would have said because he was from Palermo.

If anything, sounds help to explain something else. Subtle noises, though, which are uttered softly, like a whisper, because the loud ones are just everyday noises. There is the gramophone on the window ledge of Hotel Torino playing a song, "O sole mio", which had just been brought over from Italy. The singer's voice mixes with the shouts of the women carrying water, the cries of the fishmongers and salt sellers. There is a dromedary grunting because it has settled under a porch and doesn't want to get up. There is the boy whipping the dromedary's knees with a stick, shouting "*Tenseie! Tenseie!*" There is a local Askaro soldier with a half-Tuscan, half-Sudanese accent, who is shouting to a group of naked children, "*Kit! Kit!*" to chase them away, and one of them — a little girl — is warbling with the tip of her tongue against her palate in an ear-piercing trill. These are not the sounds which are needed now.

The only sound to listen out for is the capitano's whisper into Signora Ada's ear as he gently leans towards her, and it is why she is smiling at him, her capitano.

"I've found a buyer," the capitano tells her in his Piacenza accent, although since moving from one barracks to another he has mixed up all the Italian accents from north to south, but he knows which one pleases Signora Ada, and it sends a little shiver of pleasure down her spine, it always does, and this time too.

Signora Ada smiles and she tugs on her necklace in excitement. The buyer was the last detail, the essential one. The rest was all ready: the papers, the documents, the bill of sale. All that was missing was the old man's signature, but she was going to take care of that.

As soon as the buyer arrived in Massawa, Signora Ada was going to make over to him all the trading business of Barone Caraffa and Bros in the colony of Eritrea. Everything would be sold, all of it: Massawa, Asmara, Assab, every trading office, and sold for a good price.

Even divided in half between the brothers there would be enough left and they would return to Italy, because in Africa there would be nothing left for Signora Ada to do, and remaining under the protective wing of the barone's family was a waste of time – besides, no-one would pay attention to those imbeciles, Giovanni and Mauro. So once back in Italy, Ada would strip little Giovanni of everything, right down to his pants, inadequate cuckold that he was, a *"cornuto"*, but she said *"curnute"* with a longer second "u" because she was a country girl from Frascati.

Of course, the brothers would never have agreed to this sudden sale. Giovanni seemed resigned to staying in this forsaken corner of Africa, resigned even to dying of boredom in the place. Mauro hated it, this was obvious, he could not breathe for the heat and humidity, but he would never have got rid of the old man's assets even though he had no idea how to manage them. But what could they do? Once they saw the barone's signature at the bottom of the bill of sale they wouldn't be able to say it was false, they could not say that the syphilitic old

man was not sound of mind and body, after all those years of
pretence, making everyone believe he was still on top of things
and firmly at the helm of the company, only a bit wiser, a little
more worn out perhaps, but still in control, still doing everything. Everyone knew it wasn't true, but to declare it officially
was another thing.

And so, in the end, faced with a fait accompli, the brothers
would understand that it would be better to sell everything and
go home to Italy.

Signora Ada smiles, and in her excitement she tugs on her
necklace and the string snaps and black pebbles explode in front
of her chest, and that is how the photograph comes out, with
a galaxy of bullets blurred by movement, but it didn't matter
as the photographer knew he could touch up and colour the
image and palm it off on the Caraffa family anyway.

The photographer didn't manage to, however. The picture
turned out alright, but he never gave it to the Caraffa family,
because that very morning a certain Capitano Colaprico arrived
with two carabinieri bearing chains and arrested the whole lot
of them. And not for fraud or embezzlement, but for murder.

Above all, though, it was that the old *ferengi* knew. That he
expected it of Aster once he saw she had understood. And,
indeed, he no longer hit her.

He looked at her. With desire, but not only that.

With fear, too.

It was that fear, that sudden shudder, which sprung open

the old *ferengi*'s eye that held her back. It felt as if she were doing something bad, because she had never struck fear in anyone before.

That is what Aster thought that night, huddled on the mat, curled up like a foetus. She had a ring on her finger, a little ring, and she was sucking it like a child. From the open window a fresh breeze was brushing over her shoulders, and it would have been perfect to have slept like this, her head on her arm, had it not been for the silence.

The old man was not sleeping.

He was not wheezing. He was not catching his breath or gurgling as if suffocating in his sleep, and the silence was not like the one which preceded his nightmares – it was an awakened silence, immobile and waiting.

Aster could not do it like this.

She got up at a certain point in the night, or rather she moved to get up, and caught the reflection of the old man's eye and he was looking at her and she lay down again surrounded by the darkness of the room, on a part of the floor the moonlight did not reach.

There, she thought, if it had not been for the moonlight, maybe.

If the night had been black, as dark as her, she would have been able to lift herself up, without a sound, glide lightly on the tips of her bare toes, invisible, a slightly dimmer shadow, and reach the old man's bed, unseen and unexpected, even if he was awake.

But there was the moon, which cast bright reflections on the sweat of her skin, in the whites of her eyes and her teeth. And the planks of the floorboards would have squeaked under her weight, and the dirt would have made a scraping sound under her rough bare feet.

Aster remained in the same position for a long time, knees up against her chest, her cheek on one arm, a finger with a ring in her mouth, until she almost went to sleep.

She was startled from a subtle and painful half-sleep by the old man's rasping. He had no doubt gone to sleep too. Perhaps he had become tired of waiting. His slow and hoarse breathing had become a growl which was louder than usual, but it was the noise he made when he was sleeping.

So Aster got up from the mat and approached the bed, and the moon shone on her skin, and the floorboards creaked as she moved, and the dirt scrunched under her feet, but still the old man slept.

Aster stopped to look at him, legs laid out straight on the soaking sheet, arms stretched along his sides, eyes tight shut, the old *ferengi*, pale and naked. Then she looked around herself for something to help her, but there was nothing.

The old *ferengi* did not use a pillow.

Aster took off her dress, slipping it over her head, a light cotton dress which looked like an undergarment, and she rolled it up in her hands.

It was then that she saw the old man's eye.

It was wide open, staring at her, and it seemed as if the other eye was straining to open and look at her too. The rustling of the dress had not woken him, his eye was too alert. The old man had not been asleep, he had just been pretending. For a moment she stayed there, naked, with the dress crumpled up in her hand, so offended by the deceit that she considered getting dressed and lying down on her mat again.

Then Aster saw the look of supplication in the old man's gaze, desire, entreaty, hope and no fear at all, and so she moved fast. She leaned over the bed and with both hands pressed the dress onto the old man's face.

The old man did not move, only a twitch when the cloth covered his face, then he became still. But she felt him breathing, she felt his warm breath slipping through her fingers and the light cotton of the dress. And even though she pushed hard with the palms of her hands, it was useless, it was only going to hurt him.

Aster pulled the dress away and threw it into a corner, and stood staring at the old *ferengi*'s deluded expression as he moved his mouth without being able to speak and as he began hitting her on the arm with a closed fist, harder and harder. This time she put the palms of her hands on his face, both of them spread wide open, with her fingers gripping his cheeks to cover his mouth and block his nose.

The old man gave another jolt. He tried to remain still, but he could not. He began to writhe on the bed, and she hoisted herself on top of his body to keep him still, pinning him down, her legs over his, a sturdy girl on top of a thin old man. Despite this, his natural instinct fought back, the old *ferengi* punched her in the flesh below her ribs and fear had returned to his eye.

Aster thought about stopping, of getting off and withdrawing her hands. The barone guessed this and the fear in his eye again became a plea.

Aster pushed harder, and as that was not enough she took one hand away and clamped it around his throat, placing the side of the other open hand over his mouth, ramming it right up against his nostrils, which were again flared like that of a horse. The old man lifted an arm and grabbed her hair, he hooked a finger into the thick curls and began to pull with all his strength, and so Aster took her other hand off his mouth and squeezed it hard around his neck too, as tightly as she could, until the old man no longer seemed to spit out his tongue in an exhausted gurgling, and he stopped moving.

Aster took a step backwards. Immobile, in the light of the moon, she looked at the old *ferengi*. She stood there a long while, she did not know how long. Then she flinched. She had gripped so hard that the ring on her finger was hurting her. She took it off and flung it far into the room, sending it jangling across the floorboards.

Slowly, and gently, as if she might still harm him, Aster shut the old man's open eye and pushed his tongue back into his mouth with her finger. She covered his legs with the sheet, pulling it right up to his chest. She lifted his head and straightened it, stroking his forehead, even though she knew that now he would have no more nightmares.

She put her dress on and went to lie down in the corner, waiting for morning when she would call the signora and tell her that the barone had died in his sleep.

Aster thought she would never be able to sleep again in her life, but as soon as she leaned her arm on the mat, and her head on her arm, she dozed off.

## The drawing

The rest can be explained by a drawing on a thin piece of card. Sketched in thick strokes, as well as narrow and meticulous ones to bring out the detail, it is so compact and realistic that from afar it looks like a photograph.

It is a drawing by Signora Ada. She came top of her year at art school, and that was why she was so good at imitating the barone's signature. For a while, when she was younger, she had thought about taking up art as a career and becoming a portrait painter, because she really did have an eye for detail. Then she had met an army lieutenant from Naples, and then a student from Rome, followed by a businessman from Bari and, finally, Giovanni, whom she managed to marry, even though she had not been a virgin for some time – but that was the least of the skeletons in her cupboard.

The drawing had to be realistic, just like a photograph, because it had a particular purpose.

Its subject is Aster, naked. Signora Ada chose her because of her beautiful, curvaceous body, not unlike her own. She asked her to take off her clothes and covered her in jewels, necklaces dangling onto her bare chest and tied high at the nape of her neck so as not to cover too much. And rings on her fingers, many of them. The earrings are bigger still. There is also a glitter tiara from a dancing outfit pinned to Aster's frizzy hair.

When Signora Ada saw Aster posing in the middle of the room, her back arched, her arms alongside her body, her eyes staring down at the floor, she realized that the girl was not really like the Queen of Sheba at all, but it didn't matter, it was not a photograph and she could make up the rest herself.

In fact, Signora Ada gave Aster a sensual posture and a brazen smile, more like that of a whore than a queen, but it looked better that way. And, as she blended the black tones with the greys, sketched the details onto the paper, she was already getting excited herself, thinking of her capitano and how he had needed a bit of help recently to get himself going – it was always like that with men after a certain age. And as there were no risqué photographs to be found in the colony, and he was beginning to like the Abyssinian girls a bit too much, she had come up with the idea of doing him a little drawing from time to time, and behaving like his own little African slut too.

Signora Ada knew what would happen. Her capitano would curl the ends of his moustache with the tips of his fingers and look at the drawing with a troubled expression, as it would have made him think of her, because the posing figure did not have Aster's face. Her naked Queen of Sheba had her face, Signora Ada's features. And so the capitano would have taken her like a bitch, his hand gripping her neck like a bite, pinning her down, and she would have let him do it. Once back in Italy she would make him understand who was on top and who was underneath.

The portrait was good, very good, better than a photographic image. At the end of the drawing session, Signora Ada had asked Aster to hand her back all the jewels, and she had put them in the little chest on her dressing table: the glitter tiara, the necklaces, including the one that then broke in the third photograph, the earrings, the rings, the many rings.

Except one.

It was a ring mounted with the Asmara sun, circular on top and engraved with fine lacework. It was so light that Aster had forgotten she was wearing it on her finger, and by the time she remembered the signora had already gone off to meet her capitano and it slipped her mind again.

Then it happened that when the doctor came to certify the barone's death, a certain Capitano Colaprico accompanied him, because the two men had been together at the Caffè Roma trying to stave off the heat with a little beer. And Capitano Colaprico was good at his job. He had asked to be sent the latest criminology papers by Kraft-Ebing and Lombroso from Italy. Anyway, just seeing those black bruises on the barone's neck was enough to arouse his curiosity. So he got closer and had all the blinds removed from the windows to let light in, and, as that was not enough, he asked for the barone's body to be carried outside into the daylight, onto the veranda.

That is how Capitano Colaprico spotted the motif of the Asmara sun imprinted on the barone's ice-cold skin.

It is also why he asked the servants, discreetly, in the local Tigrinya language mixed with dialect from Puglia and Lombardy, if they had ever seen such a ring in the house before. And when one of his local colleagues, his *zaptie*, found the ring under the bed, and all of them, Asmareth, Saba – though Aster remained silent – even Signor Giovanni and Signora Ada, all of them recognized it, he understood what had happened and had the whole of the Caraffa family arrested.

"It wasn't us!"

"There is a man here strangled by a hand wearing this ring."

"It wasn't me!"

"Perhaps not alone, signora. Perhaps you needed help holding him down. He may have been old, but everyone knew he was still bright as a spark, apart from his arthritis."

"It wasn't us! Why would we have killed him?"

"To sell everything. Here are the deeds and documents ready to sign, and a telegram from a man in Italy confirming the purchase negotiations. And here is a will in which the barone leaves everything to his sons, Mauro and Giovanni, and to his daughter-in-law Ada."

"It's a fake. It was only to give us some security, in case something happened to Papa. Ada signed it."

"But you asked me to!"

"Ada wrote all the signatures!"

"With you!"

"So, I have here a fake will which makes you the beneficiaries of a man who was killed by several people, including a woman who was wearing this ring. One, two, three," – Capitano Colaprico stabbed the air with the tip of his finger, pointing at Ada, Giovanni and Mauro – "you're all to be locked up until the next steamship leaves for Italy."

Afterwards, while being interviewed by the correspondent for the *Corriere Eritreo*, who assured him he would send a telegram to Rome because he was also the correspondent for the *Corriere della Sera*, Colaprico thought back to the story of the drawing.

Signora Ada had stuttered something about Aster, the ring, a drawing, the Queen of Sheba, the capitano. But the fact was no-one had seen that drawing. The capitano had categorically denied having a relationship with the signora, and almost denied even knowing her – perhaps a little too vehemently, but that was also noted down in the statements. And Aster, in any case, was only an Abyssinian servant girl who had nothing to do with this scheming about money.

It was then that Colaprico remembered something: he remembered that when he was serving in Sardinia, first in Cagliari and then in Barbagia, he had overseen a case in Luras. It concerned the death of an elderly, sick man, and they arrested a woman with the accusation that she was a "*femmina accabadora*". She was an old lady who always dressed in black, and who lived on the edge of the village, and to whom tradition had given the task of bringing a merciful death to the sick.

She went into people's houses at night and laid the suffering person's head on her lap, she cradled them like a baby and then hit them on the forehead with her *mazzolu*, a kind of wooden mallet. Or she suffocated them by squeezing their necks between her legs. That is how, they said, the old woman in Luras carried out her task.

But that time in Barbagia, too, he had not been able to prove anything, and was forced to give up.

"So what?" he thought, despite his policeman's conscience. There was enough already to this case with its nasty greedy people, a fake will, the imprint of the ring, the motive, the opportunity: it was all clear. And besides – not the policeman in him, but the man – was also pleased it had ended this way.

They were nasty people, a really bad bunch, and they didn't belong here.

And if you don't love Africa, you don't deserve it.

That is why he smiled at the journalist and said, "So, where were we?"

TRANSLATED BY BEN FACCINI

*Valeria Parrella*

THE PRIZE

WHEN VIVIANA DIED THEY TOLD MARTA SHE HAD TO look at her mother in the coffin, otherwise they wouldn't be able to seal it.

Alessio wasn't there when they went to remove the little girl from beside the stove where she had been waiting for twelve hours. Nor was he there when they dragged Marta through the rooms of the house, one after another, their shutters folded inwards, each room muted in the way a four-year-old imagines death to be.

The local men surrounded Alessio Maranca. He was the only one, among those present in the house, who had been allowed to sleep the night before. And he had slept heavily, in the canopy bed in the guest room, everything draped and covered, the mirrors too, to make sure they did not reflect death. Alessio had gone to bed without even stopping to undress, even though the maid had, as she always did, prepared everything for him and asked him whether or not he wished for a light dinner. More exhausted by the disease that had taken his wife than heartbroken by her death, Alessio had decreed that the stove should not be turned on, not even for him, not even for an hour, and he had then let himself collapse on the bed, without putting up any resistance, while Viviana had fought with every fibre of her being to keep her eyes open, before finally dying. She had only agreed to be told about our Lord and his Calvary on earth, which would have saved her from the tortures of purgatory, because it had seemed immodest, given her circumstances, to smile and say that no, she was not yet ready to die, and that with a four-year-old girl in the house she would have very much liked to have gone on living; then she died.

Alessio shut his eyes and slept.

By dawn the local peasants had begun to bring flowers which they collected from the sides of the roads and tied into bunches with twine. They entered the house, holding their hats against their chests, happy to leave their floral offering on the piano, a real Piedmontese piano, which had miraculously escaped the bombardments of the war.

The peasant women covered their heads and moved, without stopping, straight through the reception rooms. The maid looked at their clogs or bare feet and gestured bluntly that they should clean themselves with the cloth she had left at the entrance. Like their men, the working women brought bunches of flowers, but they laid them at the foot of the body, eager to have an opportunity to admire the lace cover and the raised cast-iron bed, no doubt elevated in such a manner to make sure that mice could scurry beneath it without waking the person sleeping beneath its covers.

The ladies of the household had prayed until three, and then their murmuring of the rosary had finally quietened down, so much so that Marta could no longer hear it from her hiding place next to the stove.

Stirred from their slumber by the smell of coffee, the ladies in the velvet armchairs at the edge of the bed, watched the swollen hands of the peasant women lay bunches of flowers on the bed.

The mayor's wife followed the gaze of one peasant woman move along the corpse to the point where a corner of under-garment poked out from under the blanket, and she jumped up to readjust it, explaining to the other ladies present that "they pay more attention to the dead than they do to the brides." Fortunately, Viviana had decided on the linen she wanted in death, and it was beautiful linen that had not had to be bought on the black market during the war.

The ladies' husbands sat smoking cigars offered by the master of the house. They surrounded him and clutched him by the arm which was now marked by a black band. They talked about the city, the municipality, the streets and steps and other things that connected the city to the surrounding countryside, and they talked about the bank that had finally decided to open a branch in their small town and of the poor signora who had not lived long enough to see her husband run that bank, organize its staff and manage the capital, or even benefit from the recently increased value of the currency.

Every evening, at sunset, now that spring was making itself felt, Alessio waited for the clerk to close the bank's front door before setting off along via Pretoria – with his hat in his hand as was expected of him according to the somewhat confusing ceremonial standards commonly practised in the provinces – and he walked home, sometimes stopping to talk with new friends and their wives, exchanging comments or observations about the changing times. As he returned home every evening, Alessio missed neither Piedmont, nor his wife's presence at his side. Between her pregnancy and her illness, he had never become accustomed to her being there and had learned, out of necessity, but also on the advice of his notary, to make other plans.

The men fell silent and stood aside when the priest arrived. Alessio followed him into his wife's bedroom as the ladies increased the volume of their prayers and the intensity of their contrition. It was then that an aunt – who had come down from Piedmont on the train as far as Naples and then journeyed to the house in the back of a farmer's cart – remembered having seen Marta huddled near the stove. She found the child crying and asked her, "What are you crying for? Pray rather." Then she dragged the little girl through the rooms, and at every doorway Marta tried to hang on to something.

The spring sunshine seemed blinding after the darkness of the house. Alessio manfully held the right-hand side of his wife's coffin, while his daughter was yanked along by the aunt. He would never have held his daughter's hand in public anyway.

The presence of women in the house tapered off after a few days, but the shutters remained closed and the child dressed for mourning. Alessio swapped the black band around his arm for a more discreet black button which he pinned to the pocket of his jacket, the same pocket where he tucked his handkerchief every morning. It dawned on him that even while sick, Viviana had organized his home, orchestrating and engineering it all from her bed.

On his first Sunday alone, Alessio went to Mass at ten in the morning with Marta and the maid following him at a respectful distance, a few steps behind. The wives of the village notables, seated amongst the women to the left of the church aisle, immediately took the little girl into their care, knotting a lace veil under her chin. When the Mass was over, Alessio confirmed that he would lunch with the mayor. And he waited for the church to empty completely, and for the altar boy to begin preparing the incense for the midday service, before going into the vestry to speak to the priest while he removed his robes: "I need a mother for Marta," he said, "now."

And so it was that the priest summoned Grazia from the clay-filled fields where she was stripping wheat and explained to her that an unexpected opportunity had presented itself to her, the

only opportunity that she had had in her eighteen years of life
and certainly the first since the end of the war:

"Think of the child, speak little, don't get sick and remember that you are there in my name."


As Grazia studied the stone coat of arms hanging over the
entrance to the palazzo, she found herself wondering how old
the man she was going to meet would be, and how long she
would remain in the house and, again, hidden in the back of
her mind, what her role would be. She pondered these things
within herself, and asked nothing of the priest who was accompanying her aside from obliquely commenting:

"This is my Sunday dress, is it alright?"

"What did you want to wear – the dress you put on to work
in the fields?" the priest replied, irritably and without looking
at her because he knew she had no alternative

The maid who opened the door stared at Grazia for a long
time, starting with her feet, and then left the visitors at the front
door because she had not been expecting anyone.

That day Grazia only saw Alessio from the side as he shook
the priest's hand, and once from behind as he invited the priest
into the still shuttered living room before closing the door
behind them so that they could talk in private. Grazia remained
alone in the entrance hall. Without moving her head, she
absorbed the bottle-green velvet of the sofa, and then the carpet
that she was standing on, and also the chandelier that hung from
the ceiling like rain dripping from the olive tree outside her home.

By the time the two men had finished speaking, the priest had sewn together a family and an agreement for Grazia, neither of which she would have been able to construct herself nor even imagine being possible. Then he had said, "Sir," turning the respectful title around on his tongue, as he liked titles particularly as one had little or no use for them in their small town forgotten both by God and men, "people will soon begin to talk: keeping a young woman in your home, like this, now that you are a widower . . ."

"She is the nanny," Alessio said.

"You come from the North, here things do not work that way . . . Sooner or later you will have to marry her."

"Later then," Alessio said. "First I have to try her."

Like two cats trying to avoid a fight, or at least trying to avoid being the one to initiate a fight, Grazia and Marta looked at one another from a distance, studying each other, within their separate dens, defending the wall that separated them. That is how Grazia and Marta observed one another for the first time when it was already nightfall.

Marta let Grazia put her to bed because she was exhausted by her distress and because she understood that she could do nothing to stop it. The woman's face was completely foreign to her – her simple clothing, the smell of onion on her breath, her rough hands as she pulled the nightgown over her head: also that woman was going to sleep in her room, in the bed next to hers, and there she was, lying supine, absolutely still, seemingly not occupying any space beneath the covers. The little girl looked around herself, she looked within her thoughts and her breath for something familiar, the doll that her mother had made her, the red crayon mark on the wallpaper, her father's footsteps on the stairs as he walked towards his bedroom. But her mother had removed her doll as a punishment when she had drawn on the wall, her father, when they did meet, silenced her with the look in his eyes, and so she could not fall asleep. There was no way out, until an unexpected and deep sleep shut out her thoughts.

Grazia remained immobile in her bed without even acknowledging that for the first time in her life a sheet lay between her body and the blanket. She would have liked to have said something to the little girl, but she was not sure the child would have understood: she herself understood the Italian that was spoken in the house, but she knew she could not speak it and, in fact, in the days that were to follow, she hardly tried. She did not know what to say to Marta anyway, and before her thoughts could really take form the little girl fell asleep, then finally as she heard her breath becoming regular she turned on her side, towards the window, towards the valley that she knew so well and prayed for all those who came to mind, all except herself that is: fearful as she was to commit the sin of arrogance or indeed to feel that she was in fact in need of those prayers.

Grazia awoke at dawn as she always had. At the time previously she would have been readying herself to be collected by the foremen and their carts to go down to the fields and begin work. She needed to pee. In her new home, though, it was still the middle of the night and she had no idea how to find the bathroom alone.

Alessio's room was the first that the maid attended to after entering the house at dawn through the back entrance. The woman pressed her ear against the door to hear whether or not he was still snoring and then meandered her way to the little girl's room; here she opened the door to check that everyone was in their own bed. Often, Alessio was already up, even though his personal matters could have waited a few hours. Sometimes he smoked in bed. On other days, the rising morning heat sent him out onto his balcony as early as six, and then from the balcony he would gaze beyond the plane trees down to the ravines at the labourers whose backs would soon bear the marks of the scorching sun. Some days Grazia too started early, sorting out the girl's clothes, preparing her breakfast, and on those days the maid would find her busy in the kitchen, making use of the stove, and more than once Grazia had already dirtied the cloth she intended to use for the windows. When the maid found Grazia still in her nightdress, she reprimanded her, "Are you not ashamed? Sir will be up in less than two hours . . ."

In fact, Grazia called him "sir" and the maid "master", but only when talking to each other, as they never had the opportunity to address him directly. Alessio had likewise decided to refer to Grazia as "signora" and insisted on using the formal mode when addressing her even though the practice had pretty much fallen away in the town by then. For Alessio it was a question of both style and distance, and also a manner in which to give greater value to the money he paid her. Grazia agreed; it showed that she understood what was being asked of her and only rarely did she answer with a short sentence in which each word ended with syllables that lingered beneath her palate.

But it was Grazia's rare morning forays in her nightdress that encouraged the maid to spread untruths and tell the neighbours things she had actually never seen.

When the whispering made its way to the priest, he seized the moment to explain to Alessio that the time had come to either replace Grazia with an old nurse or make her his wife.

"*Fama, malum qua non aliud velocius ullum.*"

"A beautiful hexameter: what is it?"

"Virgil, fourth book: when Aeneas and Dido spend the night in the cave together after the storm. Reports began to spread. Virgil imagined Rumour like a monster 'with countless mouths' that could see and smell everything immediately."

"All this is absurd," Alessio said, getting up angrily and moving to look out the window. He had felt as though the arms of the chair were squeezing him too tightly. He stood watching the farm labourers transporting acidic grapes on their carts and storing them in specially designed small clay caves with doors to seal them off.

"Aeneas had indeed been in the cave with Dido."

"Aeneas himself explains, '*Tam ficti pravique tenax quam nunzia veri*'. Alessio, you see, if even Aeneas struggled with problems of this nature . . ."

"But Dido was a queen."

"The young woman is good-looking."

"Please, Carlo, don't talk nonsense."

"Stop now, come on, we are men of the world, a small world, and rather asphyxiating, a world that is still evolving, but there still is a 'society'. What is it that you are afraid of? It is a formality, a show."

"Spare me the Shakespeare."

"She would not be your wife in the biblical sense, nothing will change in your day-to-day set up, but as compensation for your effort you will have yourself a devoted and grateful servant . . . Or is this what is bothering you? Are you worried that the girl will get the wrong idea?"

"No: she is too small-minded to expect something from me."

Taking Alessio by the arm and accompanying him to the door, the notary declared loudly, "*Viresque adquirit eundo*: you will become stronger going forward." He said it more than once because it pleased him both to remember the phrase and to show that he remembered it, and he was already looking forward to returning home to his wife and telling her all that he knew over dinner.

★

Marta was the first to get in. The water almost overflowed as she lowered herself into the copper bath with the slightly rusted edges. It was a warm autumn's day and she was on a stone terrace of the house, protected from indiscreet eyes by a laurel hedge. Grazia opened a vial of Silvana water and emptied it slowly into the water and then waited for it to turn blue, as if by miracle, enjoying the subtle release of lavender scent. As a child Grazia too had bathed in a similar-looking tub, but only after many other children had gone before her. It was a ritual that depended on the master's generosity towards the labourers' children who had only well water to wash in. And it was a tradition that Viviana, as a good Christian, had taken on and made her own. Now Grazia, too, prepared the bath so Marta could enjoy it; she scrubbed her back for her and then wrapped her in a linen cloth, making her sit in the sun until her hair dried. As Marta waited in the warmth, the other children lined up, leaving their identical clothes in piles, taking their turn in the bath.

The priest came to break the news to Grazia. He had her called to the entrance hall and while she dried her hands he told her that the banker was going to make her his bride. This would happen to ensure their names were not besmirched and that the child would not be bothered with gossip when she started school. Grazia was informed of the day, the time and what was expected of her. She was also told what she should wear, what she should say and the offering she was expected to make. The pharmacist's wife would assist her. Alessio had requested this himself after confession that morning, so as to avoid any embarrassment.

The afternoon ceremony was short. The church smelled of recently cut grass. Grazia, in a sign of respect for the virginal white worn by the woman who had preceded her, wore a light-coloured suit with her hair cut in a manner more suited to an older signora even though she was only eighteen.

The maid who cut her hair barely concealed her glee, telling Grazia: "You will never be able to wear your hair long again. Your days as a young girl are over."

In return, as everybody gathered on the terrace for refreshments after the ceremony, and as soon as the opportunity presented itself, Alessio told his wife that the maid from now on should use the more respectful term of "signora" with her.

But Grazia didn't know how to savour her revenge; she understood little of what was happening around her. She stood smiling, the liqueur making her head spin, and she could not rid herself of the niggling sensation that somewhere, beyond the decorum and status of her outfit and her smile, something was missing – something that she did not have the time to look for as she took the tray out of the maid's hand and offered the pastries to the guests herself, taking the opportunity to display the ring on her finger.

This sense of loss stayed with Grazia rather like the seemingly immobile purplish cloud on the horizon that the men were pointing at with their cigars, "Tomorrow it will rain."

Grazia's cousin, and her only living relative, had come to the church during the ceremony. Without actually coming in, she had made a sign of the cross and blown Grazia a kiss from afar.

That evening before retreating to his room, Grazia's husband spoke to her for the second time that day. "Goodnight," he said. During the ceremony he had pronounced his "I do" looking at the priest.

Alessio too had been without family members at the ceremony: his sister had told him she would travel the length of Italy only for births or deaths, but certainly not to find herself in embarrassing situations.

A few days later Marta crouched down between the statues and shrubbery on the terrace and did a pee. It was the first sign of a rebellion which had its origins deep within her soul and which spilled over into her behaviour every day. Marta did not stop at disobeying Grazia at every opportunity. She decided to disobey the basic human conventions imposed on her. She stopped talking, she forgot how to hold her knife and fork, and during Mass she slipped away from her new stepmother, openly running down the aisle of the church, refusing to fit in with the world around her.

Grazia too resisted her new status; she continued to eat alone in the kitchen, sitting on a box with her plate balanced on her knees. Sometimes when Marta found Grazia sitting like this she would tip the plate into her lap and scream.

Without really understanding it, nor recognizing what he had unwillingly set in motion, Alessio observed the domestic chaos with severity. He withdrew, hoping that it would remain hidden in the home. To keep up appearances, he secured Grazia a new wardrobe and made a point of going to Mass every Sunday with both his daughter and his second wife. He walked a few steps behind them, certain that Marta would never behave as badly in front of him as she did in his absence.

Alessio and Grazia continued to sleep in separate rooms.

Grazia was never humiliated by Marta's behaviour. The fact that Marta was only five years old made no difference whatsoever in terms of the class system and its rules, all of which Grazia had taken in while growing up in the fields. It was all she knew about community life. Marta was Marta and she was Alessio's daughter. And everything in that house, from the fabrics to the furniture, all belonged to Marta. In fact Grazia belonged to her too.

Even so, Grazia gradually found a sense of authority within herself that predated these social rules, deriving as it did from a more profound order in the world. She knew what could be done and what should be avoided and what was dangerous. In her attentiveness, Grazia succeeded where Alessio failed. She knew how to look at what was in front of her and when she concentrated on something Marta said, or a gesture she had made, Grazia saw not only the little girl as she was at that moment, with her plaits and her dresses that went to her knees, she also saw her as the young and then the older woman she would become. Grazia followed Marta's every step, literally, but the care and structure she gave the child's life enabled her to gain in confidence and strength. Grazia knew instinctively when to raise her voice, she worried about the risks Marta took and was sincere in her displeasure when Marta disobeyed her rules. And when Grazia lost control and slapped the little girl, she suffered for days afterwards and immediately went and confessed her wrongdoing.

Marta hated Grazia, and with the punctuality particular to children she never missed an opportunity to tell her father about all the cruelties her stepmother visited upon her during the day – and likewise never failed to tell her stepmother that her marriage to her father was a charade. But Grazia had discovered a wealth of maternal feeling within herself that encompassed everything and that had profoundly changed her and the way she perceived herself, her priorities and her needs. For the first time in her life her personal thorn in her heart – something she had always seen with clarity and which at times she had called *God* – had become the future: the present needed all her patience.

Every night, after seemingly interminable days overflowing with perceived insults, recriminations and unexpected hopes, prickly silences and rejections, Marta went to bed with Grazia sitting immobile in the semi-darkness, like a hawk watching over her breathing.

★

Marta started trusting Grazia once Grazia started to trust herself. As she began to leave her mark on the house and feel confident enough to open the drawers and find new homes for the towels, for the sheets and the clothes. Behind, around and in front of Grazia, the house began to open up, each room renewing itself and revealing new possibilities. She discovered, among other things, that there was little point in keeping all the silver shut away in the cupboard, and that the geometric ordering of the carpets in the house could in fact be altered or that the plants on the terrace were arranged without any particular method and with no attention to the seasons.

"Look," she said to Marta who was deliberately staring elsewhere. "Look at the jasmine leaves: can you see they are looking for the sun? They are all facing the valley. The jasmine should be in flower now, but instead it is dying."

Marta did not answer.

"Look, the hortensia needs shelter from the sun; we must find it the shadiest spot in the house."

"The shadiest place is the balcony of my room."

"Well it must go there, otherwise it will die."

"I don't care if it dies."

"Neither do I, and in fact you can even pee into the flower-pot. That way it will die even quicker. But you will have to keep the plant."

"Why does pee kill plants?"

Grazia did not really know why. She remembered the fields scorched by the sun, she remembered seeing the city from below, from a distance, and she remembered how they were only allowed to move out of line and relieve themselves once work in the fields stopped at midday. Grazia remembered the onions pulled from the ground and how she ate them, still warm from the earth, with chunks of bread. She remembered the way her hands use to loosen the handkerchief tied under her chin to allow the breeze through her hair and how she used that same handkerchief to clean herself. She could see herself clearly still, crouching behind the only distinctive tree in the valley, urinating. At the same time every day. She smiled thinking how the strawberries shrivelled away. Again she thought back to how the city looked from below, from afar, from that privileged vantage point that allowed one to see things that were otherwise invisible: she imagined the city as though it were the chapel where they attended Mass; she imagined the city as though it were an infinite succession of identical chapels. In her mind, the walls rose up and enclosed only cloisters and frescoed churches. (Votive offerings of real gold.) Suddenly it dawned on her that she was there, now, inside the city, and there and then she pulled herself together. She tried to answer the little girl's questions.

"It is impossible to understand you when you speak," Marta said dragging the hortensia to her balcony.

From the moment Marta adopted the plant, she watered it every evening with own drinking water. She turned the plot plant around every morning ensuring that it grew in a balanced manner. And, in fact, two summers after its near death, it flowered for the first time. The flowers were purple and red half spheres without any smell.

"Come and see," Marta said to Grazia.

"The flowers are beautiful; next autumn I think we should move it to a bigger pot."

Alessio Maranca only realized that his second wife was twenty-eight years old when the owner of the local dairy drew his attention to the fact.

Sometimes, during that period, Alessio had people to dinner. Generally they were businessmen who were passing through and who had been to the bank earlier in the day, to request an investment or merely some advice regarding a deal they were negotiating. Because he was a northerner with no local family, they knew that they could trust Alessio to keep everything confidential. He would often invite these business-men to dinner recommending that they stay in the better of the town's only two hotels, the one that had a lobby decent enough to be used as a meeting place. The upturn in the economy, and the increase in value in the currency, had enabled Alessio to boost his trade and to be the first to succeed where others had only survived. He felt his age though. He had stopped meeting women: they too had grown older and had little to give him in exchange, and he often returned home before the bank closed. The bank was no longer a source of anxiety or stress for him, and his confidence and calm were palpable when he met with clients. This further strengthened his reputation. His guests were always men; he never invited their wives as he believed Grazia to be incapable of organizing a dinner. When Alessio was invited out, he thought long and hard about whether to accept the invitation with or without Grazia, and he turned opportunities down when he thought his arriving alone would be perceived as odd. Grazia had learned to speak a version of Italian, but as she was lacking in self-confidence her conversations were routinely transformed into a whispered litany that everyone struggled to follow. And even when no-one spoke to her, or asked her anything, not even simple questions regarding the quality of the wine, the mere thought of possibly having to contribute to the conversation left her in such a state of anxiety that she lost all appetite and, inevitably, she returned home with an empty stomach.

One evening, the owner of the dairy, with feigned nonchalance, told his host how some of his annuities came from Addis Ababa. Alessio listened with the calm assurance of a host and in the knowledge that he would have the last word, seemingly unaware that his guest's information was intended as a guarantee. Conversation between the two men was interrupted only when Grazia entered the room to serve coffee and wish her husband a good night – Alessio required her to do this every evening, even when the dinner itself was entirely served by the maid – and, after a few minutes, without any embarrassment, the guest asked Alessio if, as it seemed, his wife was in fact much younger than him.

*

Alessio really only began to think about it in the middle of the night once his initial irritation, a piqued annoyance at the provincial nosiness of his guest that he had been unable to shrug off with irony, had passed.

He thought about it. He subtracted and multiplied the duration of his widowhood, the distance that separated him from Piedmont and again his age, and when his mathematics was done, it struck him that only two rooms further down he had the perfect and legitimate solution for his old age.

Grazia had never seen a naked man before Alessio came to her bedroom. He had never wanted her help with bathing or dressing. Moreover, Grazia had pre-cut patterns that she could use with all the most fashionable fabrics, but nightshirts had never been foreseen in her dowry.

Grazia had always woken well before her husband, and now she left the marital bed early with a certain sense of relief. Yet when she went to collect Marta from school, she found herself mixing in with the other women with a profound, and entirely new, indefinable sense of pride. Sometimes Marta left her group of schoolmates and walked towards Grazia, pointing at her, saying, "Look there is my mother." Grazia welcomed her smiling and when necessary even protected her from her father who often let his disapproval of her adolescent behaviour show.

One day, while Marta was playing some Bach on the piano, the very same piano that had survived the war and the long trip from the north of Italy, Alessio left his preferred position under the window, the place where he always stood to listen to his daughter. Suddenly a feeling of contentment, the kind of satis-faction that a man feels when he only considers the present, overcame Alessio. Grazia was embroidering in the last light of the day, and Alessio walked over to her and asked, "But you, are you happy?" Grazia, who had never been happy, not even when she was Marta's age, and had no understanding of what Alessio was asking her, simply answered: "Yes," and returned to her needlework.

Alessio, however, continued to think about it all evening, and still he thought, and later again, as he moved between his wife's thighs, he told Grazia how proud he was of her and how clever she had been to guide Marta and turn her into the wonderful young woman she was becoming. He told her that she deserved a prize. He said that he would reward her with a gift, the next morning, or perhaps he would bring something back from his next trip, perhaps even a filigree ring that he had seen at a jeweller in Naples, or whatever she desired. Grazia did not answer immediately; she was surprised and too tired.

She did not speak until at dawn the answer came to her.

She waited in the bed until her husband was awake to tell him what she desired: "I would like a child of my own," she said.

That autumn Grazia often halted what she was doing, one hand on her belly, one hand on the railing for support, to watch the labourers finish work on the new railway track. She was weighed down by a sense of melancholy at odds with her condition. She observed, in her usual monotonous and flat language, that her child would speak Italian correctly and carry a beautiful Piedmontese surname. She seemed struck by this observation as though it were a thought whose import she had not previously grasped. She turned again to the new railway line and she noted that perhaps, at Easter or maybe Christmas, they would all visit Naples. Perhaps not, but one thing was certain: her child would see the sea.

Then she returned to herself and to the kitchen where she now had a washing machine that no-one in town yet knew how to use.

Alessio's sister came by train and stayed with them for a couple of months. She was the one to bring Alessio the news of the birth as the girl cleaned the birthing table and the midwife drank her coffee.

She told him, with a certain sense of apprehension, that the newborn child was a girl.

"Good," Alessio said. In that case she will be called Viviana, like my first wife.

Then he retreated into his room as the smell of lingering blood made him feel nauseous.

A few days later he gave Grazia a filigree ring.

TRANSLATED BY REBECCA SERVADIO

*Piero Colaprico*

STAIRWAY C

## Present-day London

"GRANDPA, WHAT IS DESTINY? WILL YOU TELL ME ONE OF your stories about destiny?"

Sitting on a bamboo armchair, in Bloomsbury, former carabinieri maresciallo Pietro Binda looked up from the computer screen. This grandson of his, Palmer, as they called him, was a prodigy. Once, when he was seven years old, he had asked him, "Grandpa, what's really important? To have a good life or to be remembered in a special way?"

He had answered by saying something about the importance of knowing oneself and about doing things that made you happy, "Or, if not happy, at least peaceful."

"But do you mean peaceful like the sea, which still has waves even when it's calm? Or like a mountain that doesn't worry about clouds even when they bring rain and snow? What do you think, Grandpa Peder?"

"*Ciumbia*, gracious me, what a big question . . . it's probably better to be peaceful like a sea cliff which knows that the sea will get it wet, but then the sun will come out and dry it off. No-one's life goes smoothly all the time, my dear grandson, my *nevudin*."

Now, aged nine, Palmer was asking him about destiny. Who could say, perhaps he would become a scientist, with his curious and philosophical mind. Or, maybe, like so many grandfathers, he wanted to imagine his grandson amassing an immense fortune, the grandson of a simple maresciallo. His own son had been brighter than him and left Milan, Italy and his own language to seek his fortune in computers in London. Peder did not really trust these new machines, but Umberto had been insistent: "At your age, you risked your life to put a gang of Albanian criminals in jail. The fact that you're still alive is a miracle. The doctor was clear, Papà. If you want to get back into shape, you must use your brain again, the way you do in your investigations. Anyway, unless you're completely healed I won't let you return to your mountains in Lombardy, no way. You'll remain right here with us. And if you miss home too much, I'll explain how you can get over it by using one of these ultra flat screens we're in the process of patenting . . ."

Patiently, Umberto had given his father some lessons and each morning he would leave the computer on, connected to the website of his home city's daily newspaper, the *Corriere della Sera*. In that way the old maresciallo could keep abreast of the news from Milan.

"Palmer, would you mind if we spoke later? I'm clipping on this article so that I can read it and . . ." Binda muttered.

The child came closer and helped him: "Clicking not clipping, come on, Grandpa. There, it's done, see how the next window opens? When you're finished call me," he said and went to play in his own room, as the faces of Mancini, Mourinho and the football club's president, Moratti, stared out at him from the computer screen. But the retired maresciallo was no longer reading, a thought about destiny had popped into his head. Something that had happened to him, but many years ago, when he was still part of the carabinieri.

## The last Monday of October, 1979

The light from the street lamps was weak and the telephone booth shone in the semi-darkness. In the small square, between via Lorenteggio and via Segneri, a group of idlers and gawkers kept a discreet distance. No-one wanted to be seen interacting too amicably with the carabinieri. Not even the young people from the local Arci social club were about.

The drug dealing in the nearby gardens on via Odazio, where "every bush was a hiding place for gear", had temporarily ceased. In the open-air gambling den of piazza Tirana, which was run by the lean and wiry "Ventagliatto", the unlucky gamblers would arrive in a few hours, not before, and throw their dice alongside the taxi rank.

In a corner that was not quite as dark, Binda leaned down to pick up a pair of fake tortoiseshell glasses with thick, greasy lenses lying next to a puddle of water littered with floating cigarette butts. He felt his heart stop. He knew those glasses. "I was afraid it was him, poor guy," he said to himself.

With the nail of his index finger he scratched away a lump of dust stuck to the Sellotape holding the earpiece together. "Pallina," Binda whispered.

"Yes, sir?" A vicebrigadiere who was acting as his driver

stepped forward. Of Somalian origin, he was already bald at thirty, short with a good-sized paunch.

"Pallina," Binda repeated, this time out loud. Since the other man, respectful of rank, did not feel he should say anything, the head of the murder investigation team added: "I know the man who was stabbed. Here in the Giambellino neighbourhood they called him Pallina. I knew him: a poor sod who was a bit off his rocker."

The features of the lower-ranking officer changed to express an infantile admiration. His rounded eyes opened wide, the fleshy mouth too, his nostrils widened and his eyebrows arched. A perfect actor. "None of our men were able to identify him, not even the lads in the ambulance, and you recognized him like that, just by his glasses? Then it's really true, no-one knows this city like you."

He's a bootlicker too, Binda thought, but he didn't say anything. Wrapping things in sticky tape was one of poor Pallina's habits. He even repaired ceramic plates in the same way. He used to say that he had been overwhelmed by the intelligence of the inventor of Sellotape. Pallina had lived across the street, in the housing estate.

"O.K. then, if it's only the murder of the neighbourhood idiot then we won't be working too late," the vicebrigadiere sneered.

"But what would have made Pallina leave his house at 11.00 p.m. and enter this phone booth?" Binda asked himself, without deigning to reply to the other officer who had recently arrived from Rome. Centimetre by centimetre, in silence, Binda inspected the metal floor and blood-splattered glass of the phone booth. Judging by the density of the bloodstains, Pallina had lost every drop of what flowed in his veins and arteries. "Emptied," Binda thought, careful not to disturb any useful fingerprints. The dangling receiver made him feel even more sad. "Tell headquarters we have identified the victim as Silvio Silvestri, there is sure to be a file on him. And insist with the hospital, let me know if he's still alive."

"No way he could have got out of this alive, sir," the other man said, lighting a filterless cigarette.

"Excuse me, what did you say your name was?"

"Vicebrigadiere Arturo Abdinasir, sir."

"Don't click your heels, it annoys me. When I tell you to call the hospital you do so immediately," Binda said, removing the cigarette from the man's mouth and throwing it into the puddle. Abdinasir lowered his eyes and rushed off to obey the order.

Binda looked at his watch. It was just past midnight. It would have taken a miracle to have kept a malnourished, weak man alive. And for those who were living through mourning and pain, tragedies large and small, these certainly were not years for miracles. Far from it: in fact they called them the "Years of Lead". Milan had an average of two murders every three days. There were scores being settled amongst the big gangs Francesco Turatello had tried to unify. There were also the terrorists who shot either to kill or maim. It was a constant race, morning, noon and night, following the bloodstains sprayed across the tarmac, the entry halls, the jails, the hospitals, the gambling dens and nightclubs. And, then, like this evening, in a telephone booth, where a poor Mr Nobody had been murdered. This was a case that would be closed quickly if he did not find a good lead. It often finished like that when the corpse was not important enough.

"Apparently he's dead," the Somalian vicebrigadiere spoke with his mouth full. "The nurse at the San Paolo Hospital," he continued, checking the contents of his sandwich which smelled of cured meat, "was unable to find the doctor. She said he'd gone to fetch an espresso with the head nurse and, well, given the state of your Pallina, if the doctor left him, it means . . ." He did not finish the sentence, but made a rapid sign of the cross and sank his teeth into the sandwich.

The temperature had fallen suddenly. The light rain of the afternoon had ceased, leaving a white film on the road that froze their backs. Neon lights threw shadows on the low hanging clouds hovering in the sky. Binda shivered. He had not dressed warmly enough that morning and was relieved that his wife, Rachele, was already sleeping and not worrying about him.

"Sorry about this Pallina fellow who was a friend of yours after all, no?" the vicebrigadiere said with a hint of maliciousness in his voice. Binda froze, but stopped himself from replying. His sixth sense told him that before taking any disciplinary action it would be better to get more information on the status of this officer who said that he hated Milan with all his might.

Almost all of it, because with the residual negative energy he complained about democracy and communists, a habit he had picked up from his adoptive father, a town hall clerk from Brescia, himself the son of a soldier who had volunteered for duty in Abyssinia under the Fascists. At the first occasion that presented itself Binda would remove the man from duty. In his section, you came across killers who, at the end of the day, could turn out to be decent people. And when digging around in the past of the dead, investigating those who had been rotten in life, you needed a certain amount of compassion in order to know when to stop judging.

"Did the nurse specify what type of injuries he had?" Binda asked.

The vicebrigadiere who had just opened a bottle of beer, did not understand. "Fatal injuries," he said.

"I know it's late, but you are here with the murder squad and you have to stay alert, Abdinasir. What I want to know is, exactly how was our Silvestri injured . . . ?"

"Ah, excuse me. He had the classic cuts on his hands and forearms. Your friend defended himself, but he received three stab wounds in his chest, and those were fatal, each one fatal," he replied, blowing his nose on the wrapping paper of his sandwich and throwing it on the ground. "One of the stab wounds sliced his oesophagus."

All that blood. All that pain. Someone who knew how to handle a sharp tool had bled that poor devil to death. Binda was imagining the scene of the murder and was startled to find

Cortellezzi standing next to him as though he had just come out of the telephone booth. Cortellezzi was from the mountains surrounding Varese, blond and massive, his hair in a pageboy cut; dark eyes and a large nose. He was also a good man, he was separated from his wife yet still managed to take care of his teenage children who lived with him. He also had a talent for getting people to talk, and using a local café as an impromptu barracks, he had listened to the only eyewitness, a Turkish truck driver passing through Milan with a load of almonds. According to this man, the assailant was wearing a pink T-shirt. He had noticed the struggle in the phone booth and then a person taking flight, "like a ghost", and had stopped to help after noticing that a shoe was sticking out from the two glass doors.

"Perhaps we should classify it as a street altercation between two homeless people that degenerated into a knife fight. Anyone wearing a pink T-shirt in winter . . ." the bureaucratically minded Cortellezzi said.

"We need to know who he was telephoning though."

"I have already made that request, I'm waiting for an answer from the technicians any minute now."

"Good job, Cortellezzi. If everyone was like you my work would be much easier," Binda said, reviewing the forces he had at his disposal.

The efficient and trustworthy Cortellezzi: score of seven and a half. Vicebrigadiere Abdinasir: score of double minus. The methodical Vito Pertusaro, who despite living in Milan for twenty years had not lost his Cerignola accent: score of six plus because he gave his very best, but he would never be a genius and complained about everything. There were new faces too: officers he had come across on via Moscova, but as yet he had no idea if they were competent or not. And there were some men from the mobile squad as well, one of them, Maresciallo Sebastiano Affaticati, he knew well. He had been in the anti-terrorism unit in Florence for three years and he could handle every situation. Score: between seven and eight, if he was in the mood to work and there were not any attractive women in the vicinity.

"Cortellezzi, round up the boys. We're going to have a brainstorm."

"Yes, sir."

Binda gathered the men around the telephone booth. Even the most expert among them liked an operational meeting on the street. If you had already worked on solving a hundred murders it would be pretty serious if you didn't know what to do. For some of the officers, Binda knew, it was better to tell them what to do. For others, though, it was gratifying if they were able to suggest something intelligent in front of the entire team. The ideal was that each man understood he was part of a team that depended on him, not because of rank or seniority, but rather because he knew his trade properly. Binda pointed to a balcony on the second floor: it was full of sculptures, an assemblage of bicycle parts, cutlery and balloons. He explained that Silvio Silvestri, nicknamed Pallina, had not always been a difficult man. He had been a teacher at a secondary school in Milan. A young female colleague had abandoned him on the eve of their wedding: "Apparently she ran off with a rich industrialist from Novara, the divorced father of one of the students."

Silvestri had attempted suicide and fallen into a chronic depression for which he had not sought treatment. Binda did not understand how, but the school in question had not fired Silvestri, rather they had downgraded him from faculty member to janitor. He had not survived long, and ended up spitting in the face of a former colleague who humiliated him by sending him off to wash his car. After which he had been fired.

Binda observed his men. Now, for them too, Pallina was no longer just some poor crazy bastard murdered in a telephone booth by another deranged person. Binda continued, "he was fifty-three and for the past fifteen years he lived alone, he was called Pallina because he always held a tennis ball and would bounce it on the street in front of him. Sometimes he would give a ball away to a passer-by, signing it with the letters S.S., a play on words – his own initials, but also those of the province where he was born, Sassari, in Sardinia. Those pseudo-sculptures that you see on his balcony were inspired by the lightness of Bruno Munari's work and by a quote from the artist: 'the greatest obstacle to understanding a work of art is the desire to understand it.' Pallina was no fool: he was a man who had been brought to his knees by destiny. And while he was kneeling, he was given the *coup de grâce* by somebody. So, let's go and have a look at his flat; maybe we'll find something useful. Ah, there's another fact that I need to tell you, I almost forgot," he lied.

"The neighbourhood priest," Binda said, starting to climb the steps, "described Pallina as a devoted parishioner with a strange habit. Some Sundays, after Mass, he would stop on the church steps and give a speech or even reprimand people." Which was how Binda had come to know him. Pallina, he recalled, as he entered the iron door of the housing block, had had the foolish courage to point an accusing finger at the "Seven Dwarfs", as the short-statured male family members of a Calabrian clan were nicknamed. Owners of a café in Baggio, they were involved in kidnappings and assassinations. "Pallina once shouted from the church steps, 'Repent! What are you doing in church if you then go and torment people?' There followed an attack by a sort of Calabrian 'Grumpy' in the *'ndrangheta*, using an iron bar and a screwdriver. This sent Pallina to hospital where he hovered between life and death. Once out of his coma, Pallina had repeated the accusation, but had not wanted to sign the police statement, so we had to use a generic charge of assault. In the end we were able to get that delinquent six years for assault with intent to kill."

"So then, your friend should almost say thanks to his assassin," the Somalian vicebrigadiere said, the first to arrive at the victim's front door. "It sounds as if he had wanted to check out for some time and now he's finally done it."

"Be quiet, African, the man had balls and merits respect," Pertusaro snapped.

\*

The door was ajar. A large pot of minestrone was still cooking over a low flame. A floor lamp was on. A recently published book, *Falling in Love and Loving*, was lying on a sofa bed and open in the middle – the subject of the book was the cross which poor Pallina bore.

"You can tell he raced out of the house," Affaticati said, tucking a rebellious curl behind his ear.

"Taking this with him," Cortellezzi added. He had joined them, out of breath. He held up a half-broken tennis racket. "The patrol boys just came back from the hospital with his personal effects, nothing noteworthy unfortunately." He handed over a plastic bag filled with the contents of Pallina's pockets. A wallet with a few small-denomination banknotes, two church postcards, one of Sant'Antioco of Bisarcio, the other of San Nicolò of Trullas, and a pack of breath-freshening mints.

"And, maresciallo, this is good. Guess who Pallina was calling? Us, someone at the station, maybe it was you," Cortellezzi said.

"The telephone technicians told you that?" a surprised Binda said.

"Yes, they worked it out and the first numbers were 627 ... but then Pallina wasn't able to finish off dialling the 61."

"Do me a favour – what was it you said your name was?" Binda asked the Somalian vicebrigadiere.

"Arturo Abdinasir, sir," he snapped to attention. Contemptuous with the rest of the world, but most formal with his superiors.

"Don't click your heels, Abdinasir. Contact headquarters again. Tell them we need Forensics here quickly and ask for two reinforcements from the mobile squad."

"Maresciallo, there's no phone here," Cortellezzi interrupted.

"Eh, right, of course. Otherwise Pallina wouldn't have entered the phone booth of death outside," Affaticati added.

"He had something urgent to tell us. But who killed him to prevent him from talking?" Pertusaro said, rather redundantly, as he walked in circles around the one-room apartment, with a sort of Sherlock Holmes look about him.

"But, first of all, let us imagine the scene: he was here cooking and reading. Why would he have suddenly gone down to the street with a tennis racket in his hand, smashing it over the head of the person who then probably killed him?"

"Maybe he remembered something or had a sort of epiphany or . . ." Affaticati suggested.

"Or he heard something, in here, inside the apartment," Cortellezzi said.

"An internal voice in that unscrewed head of his, or a real voice?" asked one of the officers who had just arrived on the scene.

"Let's just be quiet a moment," Abdinasir suggested.


After a few seconds of silence Binda had had enough and went to the door that led out onto the long balcony in the shape of a zigzag. These housing estates never ceased to amaze him. He had solved a double murder in via Lopez in the Oggiaro quarter where the courtyards were a no-man's-land. Looking for a pistol, he had broken through a house wall in via Novate that crumbled like a cracker. He had clambered up a dark stairwell in via Monte Faltrona chasing a transvestite who had raped and almost killed a client. He had gone into the warren of housing estates in Comasina looking for Renato Vallanzasca, the gangster who bragged that girls "waited for him with their panties between their teeth".

And now, in the heart of the Giambellino estate, on via Lorenteggio, he could not help but think that the architect had revisited the traditional gated houses of Lombardy and given them a penitentiary twist instead. Rather than wrought iron there were blocks of reinforced concrete. Instead of classical wooden doors there were squared-off entrances like those of a medieval fortress. And the balconies, rather than just simply curling round the door of each neighbour, were designed as passages that, between twists, turns and straight lines, ensured that every stairway butted up against the stairway next to it. The housing development looked like a vertical labyrinth. "You know, I think the architect robbed this design from an Escher print," Binda said. He had always asked himself why the mayors of big cities boasted of having given housing to the poor. They had actually given them *Lagers*.

Perhaps it was true what people said, that politicians, business men and architects were all in cahoots in order to steal as much as possible. Projects, contracts and worksites in exchange for bribes. A gigantic rip-off that damaged the lives of everyday people; but no, he did not even want to consider that the world actually worked in this way.

Binda raised his eyes. There were few lights on in the concrete Swiss cheese, people were asleep or faking sleep. Few were aware of Pallina's murder or of the arrival of the carabinieri. They might have heard the ambulance siren, but had not given it too much thought. Screaming sirens in this neighbourhood were all too frequent. And then, increasingly, it seemed, people were closing their doors on the outside world. Binda knew just how difficult it was to find witnesses in Milan.

"Men, excuse me, but in my opinion, someone who lived in a place like this could only be accosted by another person who lives in a place like this," Binda said.

"I was thinking the same thing," Pertusaro added. "Let's look for any traces the murderer may have left behind. I reckon he would have had to have left some bloodstains on his way back from the telephone booth."

Binda called Cortellezzi over. "We have to proceed by the rules if we want to solve this case. Put someone out front, at the main entrance, and at the rear too. Ask them to identify everyone coming in or going out. Abdinasir, you and Pertusaro are to comb every square centimetre of Pallina's apartment. When you've finished," he said to Cortellezzi, "join me at the caretaker's lodgings. Let's see if there is someone who can accompany us so the tenants don't become alarmed when we wake them. That way we'll lose less time."

"Who are we going to wake up?"

"What do you mean, who? Everybody, that's who. We'll start with the ground floor where Pallina lived and then move to the first floor and then upwards. This will be a door-to-door operation, there's no other way."

"What should I be doing?" Affaticati asked, eyeing himself in the mirror to check how the jacket of the new uniform fitted him.

"You've got instincts, use them. Look around you. I want every clue possible," Binda said.

"These housing estates smell of victory," the Somalian vice-brigadiere said ironically.

Seeing the maresciallo's puzzled face, Cortellezzi explained, "it's a line from a popular movie that's just come out, my kids use that phrase too."

"I saw it myself, 'Apocalypse Now', it's about Vietnam, actually about Cambodia," Affaticati said.

"In twenty years this place will be exactly the same; they'll use those chemicals here too, naphthalene acid and palmitic acid," Abdinasir said.

"Say that again?"

"Napalm, investigations will be a thing of the past, they'll have to level entire zones . . ." He was no longer being ironic: it was stated as though it were simple fact.


The caretaker for the housing estate was half asleep in front of her T.V. and took several minutes to throw a camel-hair coat over her dressing-gown. She looked like a witch with her red curly hair, curved nose and protruding teeth, all this combined with painted white nails. And she knew how to be deliberately vulgar when she opened her mouth: "What are you saying, that stupid ass of a Sardinian nutcase . . . ?"

"Could there be someone in this building who had a grudge against Signor Silvestri?" Binda asked her.

"As far as I know that signore argued with everyone . . . but me, commissario, I mind my own fucking business."

"I'm not a commissario, I'm a maresciallo, and if you don't mind, please speak in an appropriate manner. Are there any criminals living here?"

"Define what you mean by criminal."

"Someone who has been in jail or is involved in criminal activity or is aggressive with other tenants."

"No, we have good folk here, even the drug addicts on Stairway C aren't bad, they only sell to the people who come looking for it and they always sell outside our courtyard. As long as I'm here there won't be any dealing."

"The drug addicts in Stairway C . . ."

"Are squatters, obviously. You probably know that about ten apartments are occupied by families who have been evicted elsewhere. There are also a few on unemployment benefit, a few young people . . ." the witch said as she listed her tenants.

"How many apartments are the squatters occupying exactly? Are you sure there are only ten?" Cortellezzi asked sharply.

"Yes, more or less, maybe a few more than that," the care-taker admitted.

"Shouldn't you have a list of the squatted apartments?" Cortellezzi was unbeatable when it came to knowing regulations.

"Actually, I have one here somewhere."

"Signora, how many stairways are there?" Binda asked.

"All together?"

"No, a few at a time."

The woman sighed, she scratched her forehead with her white fingernails. "On this side there are eight, they go from A to H. On the other side there are also eight and there they go from L to S."

"Yeah, right, we've even got L.S.D. stairways," Cortellezzi snorted.

"And every stairway has five floors and each floor has from four to six apartments, does that suit you, commissario?"

"You still don't get it – he's a maresciallo. This means that there are between two hundred and twelve to three hundred and eighteen households," Abdinasir calculated with surprising rapidity. He had just finished inspecting Pallina's modest cubby-hole, together with Pertusaro. Neither had found anything of interest. No-one checked to see if the maths was correct.

"I don't believe this," Binda said, watching Affaticati as he crossed the courtyard in energetic strides, smoking one of his small cigars, talking with a tall, slender, attractive forty-year-old. The uniform on the mobile squad officer had all the elegance of a tailor-made dinner jacket.

"Lucky him, he was born to be chased by women," Cortellezzi shrugged, admiring the woman with the subtle nose of a model, short black hair and a perfectly formed mouth. She had thrown a leather motorcycle jacket over her long red dressing gown.

"Signora Astrid lives alone on the ground floor and was telling me that she heard screaming coming from the street, and because she was worried she opened the windows and looked outside. Unfortunately her windows don't look out directly on the telephone booth, I checked," Affaticati said.

"Do you hear screams very often?" Binda asked the new arrival.

"Not that often, but it's also not entirely rare that I do. Between piazza Tirana on one side and via Odazio on the other, every now and then an argument occurs, but here on the housing estate it's rather quiet," Astrid said with a seductive smile, her voice low and honeyed. Affaticati could not keep his eyes off her. The leather motorcycle jacket barely contained her ample Sophia Loren-like breasts.

"Signora Astrid, in your opinion, did Signor Silvestri have any enemies?" Binda asked.

"Poor guy, no, he didn't bother anybody, though he did have a nasty habit of eavesdropping at people's doors, didn't he?" she said to the caretaker, who nodded, a little annoyed.

"If a husband and wife were having trouble, sooner or later, he would spy on them," Astrid told them. "He was a sort of collective conscience. I work in fashion and he would tell me that I transformed women into prostitutes and that was the reason why my house was more beautiful than anyone else's and why I was divorced." She smiled.

"Had he argued with anyone recently?"

"His latest invectives had been directed at the orthodontist who lived on the fourth floor. When his wife was out, the orthodontist would bring his nurse over, she dresses like one of those girls from the Formula One races, with everything showing."

"How did it end?"

"The wife is still here with the kids, and the orthodontist went to live in via della Commenda with 'Miss Unbuttoned Shirt'. In any case, neither he nor anyone else ever raised a finger against that poor nutcase. You guys didn't know him, but he was short – as thin as a rake. He should have been a jockey."

"Yeah, if only one could have found him a horse as crazy as he was," Abdinasir laughed alone.

The carabinieri divided the work up. A few of them went to Stairway C to roust the drug dealers from bed. There were three of them, all young, and they were flustered by the police bursting in. During the search of their apartment, however, they were at ease, none of them was stupid enough to keep any "gear" in the flat. Their stash was elsewhere. Other carabinieri knocked on the doors closer to the apartment of the former teacher.

No-one had heard or seen the slightest thing; not even the

two retirees, nor the muddy young couple who appeared to have just returned from a camping trip. The train engineer for the Milan–Lecce line hadn't seen anything either. Other tenants had come out onto the stairway, some timidly, others raising their voices. As soon as they heard the fuss was about the murder, about Pallina being killed, they shrugged, "that guy was crazy as shit, we don't know a thing."

"Binda, sir, over here."

Cortellezzi had called him, he was holding the arm of an elderly woman with blue streaks in her hair. She was crying, her false teeth were missing, "my granddaughter Dores, my Dores," she repeated, standing on the first steps of the stairway. Despite the humid cold of the evening she was in her bathrobe; on her feet were a pair of absurd hairy slippers decorated with the face of Pluto the dog. He seemed to be biting her bony ankles. "Dores didn't come to say hello and she always does on Mondays when she gets home, I didn't think anything of it until I heard you all. You woke me up and a sense of anxiety overcame me, I felt my heart snap shut and I'd like to know if she has come home . . ."

The climb up the stairs, the cold, and the anxiety eating away at her, had robbed the old lady of breath and made it difficult for her to speak. The beautiful Astrid came out of her apartment on the ground floor with a progressively more dishevelled Affaticati at her heels. She was carrying a glass of water which she offered to the grandmother.

"Thank you, dear, please stay close to me, you're a friend of Dores." She could barely talk, her gums grinding.

"Don't worry, Bianca, I'll stay with you, I'm here to help," she said, trying to reassure her.

"Signora, would you mind lending her your jacket?" Binda asked.

Astrid shook her head. "In a week I have the fashion shows, if I get sick now I'm done for, but wait a minute." She turned around and went back into her apartment, returning with a synthetic fur coat the colour of sunset. "Sebastiano," she said, raising her voice.

And Affaticati, with a caring and charming smile on his face, jumped to help the forty-year-old wrap the warm fur around the grandmother's shoulders. In a second she was dressed in the latest Milan fashion. "Here, allow me," Affaticati said with great delicacy. "Actually, since you're here, Signora Astrid, would you mind leaving me your phone number? You never know, it's for the investigation," he added, taking a notebook out of his pocket. Turning his back to her, he winked at his colleagues as the woman leaned on him, slowly taking the pen in her hand. And as though it required concentration, she wrote her telephone number and full name at the top of the page. The letters were crooked and written with a trembling hand: De Magistris, Astrid. Strange, Binda thought, observing with interest Affaticati's blatant attempt to put the move on her. Someone who speaks so well, but writes so poorly. Maybe she just says she works in fashion, who can know?

"Perhaps I'll take these officers to your granddaughter's apartment myself. Do you have the keys?" Astrid said as she gave the notebook back to Affaticati.

"I left the apartment open, you can go in. I'm too afraid to . . ." the grandmother replied. With the orange-coloured fur coat on, she seemed to lose all seriousness.

The young woman's apartment was located right under Pallina's, one room with a mezzanine. Something serious had happened there, something very serious.

"Son of a bitch!" Abdinasir shouted.

The mattress on the bed was partially burned; the ashes were still smoking from a fire that had been smothered. There was a red curtain on the floor, the cords ripped out, and a broken curtain rod lay next to it. There were clothes everywhere. Some yellow knickers were dangling from the stove in the kitchen, like a wet flag. On the arm of the couch, and on several paper tissues, there were streaks of clotted blood. A butcher's knife was twenty centimetres from the kitchen sink, as though it had been rinsed and dropped, as though it had been scalding hot.

"Don't touch a thing."

"Of course, sir."

"Signora, do you also know . . . ?"

"Yes, well enough. Her name is Dolores but she's called Dores. She works as a beautician in a hairdresser's on via Foppa, she's been living here for the past six or seven months. She had come to visit her grandmother and found out that this apart-

ment was vacant, so she broke down the door. The legal tenant
was dead anyway."

"Sure, why not? I've been on the waiting list for a housing
estate apartment for three years. This is an example of why the
waiting list is worthless," Cortellezzi said.

"But Dolores is not a bad person," Astrid said, in a firm but
polite tone of voice. "She pays the housing estate her rent every
month, she pays her utility bills too."

The Dolores in the photograph on the wall had a very
sweet face, long, straight blonde hair, a round but well-shaped
nose and light-brown eyes; perhaps the lips were a bit thin.

"She's beautiful," Abdinasir said, removing the silver-framed
photograph off the wall and staring at the young woman's
image, without the slightest worry about fingerprints. Dolores
was sitting on a large rock by the sea, smiling, with her fringe
across her forehead. She was holding a freshly caught squid in
one hand.

"She's a serious woman," Astrid said, grabbing the frame
and replacing it on the wall.

Grandma Bianca had not wanted to return to her apartment
alone and was practically leaning on Astrid, wringing her hands
together with worry. Astrid was exchanging alarmed looks
with Affaticati.

"Do you have any idea who might have done this, signora?"
one of the carabinieri asked.

"My granddaughter was keeping company with a client

from the place where she worked, but I don't know any more than that. She's a good girl. She went to London after failing her exams, but she has her head on straight. Though I always say it's not the same around here now. I saw the bombings during the war, I was a worker in via Forze Armate, but there was a lot of dignity in our poverty, that's what I always say. Nowadays all you have to do is see who is living in these apartments to know that the world is spinning backwards; instead of workers they put drug addicts in here. Where will it all end? What future does my Dolores have in a world like this?"

The team of detectives studied the apartment, the positioning of possible weapons in the sink; they looked for clues to Dolores' fate. Binda's attention was drawn, more than by the knife, or the broken curtain rod and the smouldering mattress, by an object that seemed out of place in this particular apartment: a very new, costly German washing machine that dominated the kitchen. "Who brought this in?"

Astrid didn't know, neither did the grandmother. The caretaker had joined them with the list of squatters and the apartments they were in. She shrugged, "I haven't seen any delivery trucks lately. This one sure is a beauty, I'd like to have a washing machine like that," she said, fingering the dials and buttons.

"Excuse me, maresciallo. Maybe Dores had a car . . ."

"Yes, an old red Fiat 128," Astrid said, heading down to the street, followed by the caretaker, Cortellezzi and Affaticati. She spotted the car immediately and pointed it out. The car, a 1969 model, was parked about twenty metres from the housing estate entrance against the kerb. There were two stuffed toys inside and a little drawing of two entwined hearts. In the ashtray was a stubbed-out Muratti cigarette.

A beauty-case contained a pack of six condoms with only two left. Under the seat there was a tennis ball signed S.S.; Dores and Pallina knew each other. Before it had been just an obvious theory, but now there was confirmation.

"This murder, double or single, has to be solved now, otherwise, given the environment we're in, we'll never get to the bottom of it," Cortellezzi said, tossing the tennis ball with the S.S. to Binda.

"In my opinion we have one possibility. We have to keep working on the tenants, we have to identify all of them and we have to do it quickly. We also need to ask for reinforcements."

"The maresciallo is right. But how are we going to do it in this huge warren, with how many families?" Pertusaro asked, scratching his chin.

"At least two hundred families," Abdinasir said.

The maresciallo held his hand up, "Arturo, you're good at arithmetic, so you keep count of who is here and who isn't, who has been interviewed and who hasn't. Knock on every door. If no-one answers put a sign up telling people not to enter and to call us. And at the bottom of every stairway I want an officer in uniform. Stairway by stairway, is that clear? Pertusaro, you forget about the tenants, you have only one thing to do, worry about that new washing machine. Find out who bought it."

"They have serial numbers you can use to discover where it was purchased and how it was paid for," Cortellezzi added.

"Signora, you can return to your lodgings, but leave us that list of tenants," Binda finished off by saying.

"What about me?" Astrid asked.

"Maybe you could make us all a coffee?" Affaticati said tentatively.

"That would be great, I'd willingly drink an espresso. Who can think about sleeping tonight?" Grandmother Bianca said, not letting any of them out of her sight.

With the noise of doorbells ringing, and footsteps up and down the stairs, the other tenants had been awakened. The news of Pallina's murder and Dores' disappearance was racing from one floor to the next. But the knowledge was not causing much unrest, as though each apartment were a ship alone on high seas. Some of the tenants, inside their kitchens with the carabinieri, had decided to tell the real story of everyday life within the housing estate: "Stairways B, C, H, M and N are where the squatters live and the caretaker is on their side. The trouble started when the old caretaker retired and this one arrived to take his place. People steal from the mailboxes and even clothes drying outside disappear."

"These apartments weren't like this before this caretaker arrived: she's from Agrigento in Sicily and she's in the apartment-squatting racket."

"I'm even afraid to go outside. My neighbour Clementina

. . . well, she had to go into hospital for a hip replacement and they stole everything. While she was gone two families from Caserta took over her apartment. They had to be evicted by the police. A little while later a man from Calabria moved in and he doesn't talk to anyone."

"Here the problem is drugs. The dealers from via Odazio are supplied by someone who lives in these apartments. Who, I couldn't say. But, please, maresciallo, don't get me in trouble here. I have a sixteen-year-old daughter and I can't risk anything happening to her."

Huge raindrops started to fall, one by one, first just a few here and there. Within a few minutes a downpour forced everyone to take shelter. In some cities the rain smells of earth, in others it smells of woods. In that area of Milan it smelled of crushed insects. Night and day were beginning to merge. Binda had let his men work, limiting himself to listening to the main bits of information and taking care that no-one got through the net. That is until a young officer in uniform, with a triangular face and a goatee sculpted on his chin, called out to him, "Maresciallo, can you come to the car? They're looking for you on the radio."

"Who is?"

"Capitano Notarbartoli."

Notarbartoli and the maresciallo did not think much of one another. "With what authority did you order all these men to help in this investigation? I said to myself, maybe he has caught Moretti with the Skorpion gun that killed Moro, maybe he's organizing a round-up in one of the gambling dens of Epimonda, but instead you're all down in via Lorenteggio for the death of some down-and-out? What's got into you? You can send them all back here immediately in case there's a real emergency, and then you can write me a detailed report."

"No, capitano, I'm not sending anyone back to headquarters, I need every man here, I'm combing through a housing estate with over three hundred families."

"Are you refusing to obey an order? Over."

"I'm simply trying to do my job. Over."

"Over my arse, explain yourself better."

"This guy, Pallina, is killed as he's telephoning the police station in via Moscova. We entered an apartment directly under his and found it ransacked. The woman who lives there is nowhere to be found. If two plus two still adds up to four, someone was harming the young woman in question and Pallina became aware of it and was sounding the alarm, and he was prevented from doing so. And to stop him, they killed him. Then the killer took the woman with him, we don't know if she's alive or dead. Over."

"How old is she? And who is this woman? Over."

"Twenty-two years; she's a university student," Binda lied. If he had said that she was a manicurist and a squatter in a housing estate perhaps nothing would have changed, but maybe it would have. "So, now you understand, capitano? That's why I didn't bother you with this, I knew you would have acted in the same way if you had known all the facts, which they still don't know at headquarters."

"You have a kidnapped woman or a murdered woman? Or is she the one who killed Pallina? Over."

This capitano was a pain in the neck and Binda could not cut the conversation short as he wished to. "I only know that in an emergency we're the ones who are on duty, there are too many closed doors . . ."

Notarbartoli's response caught Binda by surprise, "Alright, keep on it, but how are we going to cover the rest of the day's shifts? Who is going to cover for me next Sunday? Over."

Binda and the young carabinieri with the goatee looked at each other for a second. The hands of the younger man were on the steering wheel of the car; the rain beat on the vehicle's roof. For some of the higher officials all of them were simply numbers to put into the on-duty slots.

"If there's another situation, even if I'm off duty I'll cover it," Binda suggested resignedly. "But leave me the men, at least until 2.00 p.m. Over."

"Do you have half a lead or are you basing this entirely on what you might find entering the apartments?"

"I have a washing machine, over and out."

"Luigi Verga is the name of the man who purchased the washing machine," Pertusaro told his colleagues. It was 9.15 a.m. and he had just returned to the scene in the squad's Alfa Romeo with the siren screaming, though he did not enjoy speeding, even when on duty. In those years, more than terrorism and organized crime, he hated politicians; and he frequently had to act as bodyguard for them. "My dream," he used to say in his Pugliese accent, "would be to turn round and clap handcuffs on them. They're despicable, even to go and pick up their lovers from the hairdresser they make us speed at a hundred kilometres an hour."

Pertusaro rubbed his cheeks with satisfaction, he had found where the washing machine was purchased with two telephone calls. The person in charge of sales for the German appliance manufacturer in northern Italy had told him. Having intuited the urgency, the man used a hyperactivity worthy of both Teutonic organization and native Brianzolo stubbornness to solve the riddle. He had done the research himself amongst the distributors and shops and, thanks to the serial number, was able to give Pertusaro the name and address of the wholesaler who had cashed the cheque of a certain Luigi Verga.

The carabinieri passed the photocopy of the buyer's identity card between themselves: twenty-nine years old, born in Romano Banco, resident in Busto Arsizio, profession artist.

"Shall we go and pick him up?"

Binda raised his right hand. "Hold on a second, what did we say before? That whoever created this mess could very well be here, so going all the way to Busto Arsizio could be a waste of time. First let's take a quick look right here." Together with

Pertusaro, he went and knocked on the caretaker's door, waving the photocopy of the identity card under her nose.

"Have you ever seen this person around here?"

The redhead, dishevelled, with sleep still crusting her eyes, almost fainted on seeing the photo. "What the . . . was he the one who did all of this?"

"Answer the question. Do you know this man?"

"Yes commisario . . . I mean maresciallo. That's Gino, he lives on the third floor of Stairway E with a woman. I don't know if they're married, but they have two children," she hastened to add.

Pertusaro was impressed. "Thank you, maresciallo. That saved us a useless trip."

"Go and get Verga up and keep him wondering what's going on, don't say a word about Dores. Bring him to the girl's apartment, I want to see the expression on his face," Binda ordered. The Forensics had just shown up: "better late than never." In next to no time they had taken fingerprints, put traces of organic material in plastic bags and taken photographs of the minuscule apartments.

Binda really wanted an espresso, he had been on his feet non-stop for many hours without eating or drinking anything.

He stopped in the courtyard, staring at Pallina's open door, poor man, bled to death. Binda's thoughts took him back to a lengthy discussion he had once had with Pallina regarding two boxers, Nino Benvenuti and Sandro Mazzinghi. Pallina was a staunch supporter of Benvenuti and had gone to see his famous match against Mazzinghi back in the days when boxing was so popular and important that a ring had been erected inside the soccer stadium of San Siro.

It was 18 June, 1965, and there were forty thousand fans there. Pallina was still a teacher then and also giving private lessons. He earned enough to buy tickets directly under the ring, some of the best seats. Binda had also gone to San Siro that night, but he was up in the stands, using a mariner's telescope to see the action.

So both of them had seen the sixth round with their own eyes, the round in which Mazzinghi, the champion, was knocked out by the punches of the fighter from Trieste. Though afterwards they were unable to reach an agreement in their analysis of the fight.

Binda justified the defeat: "Mazzinghi was seriously injured a year and a half ago in a car accident in which his wife died, you can imagine his state of mind. But since they offered him twenty-two million lire for the match – he was the reigning champion after all – he accepted and lost. But, as you know, in 1968 he reclaimed the title of world champion, and he did so beating Kim Soo Kim, the same boxer who beat your Nino Benvenuti."

"Benvenuti trained for months, he had experimented in the gym with a surprise punch against middle-weight sparring partners and knocked them to the mat. During the fight it had worked perfectly, his right uppercut was strong enough to bring a bull to its knees and Mazzinghi was a colossus with clay feet, as everyone knew. The match at San Siro was a work of art and proof that Benvenuti was not only more refined technically but also stronger and more of a man."

"More of a man . . ."

They had spoken of honesty and uppercuts, of boxers and Plutarch. Pallina, a man life had used as a punch-bag, was a passionate follower of the boxing ring, of fighters and good literature. Binda regretted the times he had been discourteous to Pallina, when colleagues had called him to announce the arrival of the poor man who refused to enter the police station. But what would have changed? "It was as if destiny had picked on Pallina to harm him." His life was like a pinball game, banged and battered from one flipper to another, before sliding inexorably out towards the "Game Over" slot.

"But, my old friend, now I'm going to make myself a coffee at Dores' house and then I hope to make it to your funeral. As soon as I manage to send to trial the bastard who knifed an old sentimentalist like you. And maybe I'm one too," Binda thought as the voice of a woman vibrated in the courtyard: "Gino didn't do anything. Gino, tell them. Where are you taking him?"

Binda waited for a burst of simulated sobbing; it didn't happen. Palmira, the wife of Luigi, a.k.a. Gino, cursed the officers, "fucking cops," but was not about to cry in front of them.

Brigadiere Pertusaro was standing next to her and looked at the woman's face with the expression of a rock climber about to tackle a difficult route. He did not see any footholds. There was a little chance of success. And yet he had to get to the top.

The bony woman with blue eyes still swollen from sleep and teeth stained by caffeine and nicotine swore that her husband had not moved from their apartment. "Since the news came on at 8.00 p.m. Gino hasn't left the house."

"Signora, you know, don't you, that relatives aren't allowed to tell lies in a police investigation?"

"What lies? It's the truth. I was there. He watched the news on T.V."

"And afterwards?"

"Well, afterwards, after . . . Let me think a minute."

Gino Verga did not look so good. His matted grey pyjamas matched the spectral colour of his skin. His eyes were recessed, his forehead high, with salt-and-pepper hair combed back. He was thin with a protruding stomach; a thick gold chain round his neck held a tiny diamond. The large gold-and-steel watch worn on his skinny right wrist would have sufficed for a year or two of rent.

"What happened?" he said, observing the devastated apartment.

"Did you know Dores?" Binda asked as he prepared the coffee maker.

"Can I call my lawyer before answering any questions?"

"You may call anyone you wish if I accuse you of something, or if you incriminate yourself. Are you telling me that you killed this woman and that before her, you killed Pallina? Is this what you're telling me?"

It was difficult to tell if Verga became more pallid at this point, but his lower lip began to tremble.

"If you're telling me you killed someone, then call your lawyer. You must know where the phone is in this place."

. "I haven't killed anyone, and you woke me up at dawn."

"It's after 9.30 a.m."

"For me that's early, and what is this mess here?"

"We're sorry if you're so sensitive. Did you know Dores?"

"Excuse me, but if my lawyer isn't present I cannot respond, isn't that right?"

"Do you have a criminal record?"

"One offence, six years ago. I'm practically clean."

It took five minutes, and all of Binda's patience, offering him a cup of coffee, to convince Gino Verga to quit beating about the bush.

"Yes," Gino admitted, "I've known her since school, since she went to school I mean. We fell out of touch until she moved in here, in the same building. It was a coincidence."

"Right, both of you ex-students and both of you squatters. Is that all? Any other coincidences that bind you together? Affaticati asked.

Cortellezzi had stopped his rounds amongst the tenants and entered the apartment. He came up close to Binda and whispered in his ear.

"They're telling me that this subject here is the head of the squatting racket." Perhaps he hadn't spoken softly enough, or maybe Verga realized that he could not hide all the facts, and at that point he said, "Alright. Dores found this place thanks to me. I got her in by knocking the door down."

"But your wife doesn't know that you're old schoolmates, does she?" Pertusaro, who had just returned to the apartment too, said raising his voice. "I've been interrogating her until now. She says he was at home all evening, doing what, she couldn't say. She also said that he always got along well with Pallina and that he didn't so much as say good morning or goodnight to this blonde here. A bit strange, no?"

"What's strange about that?"

"You live just a few stairways away from one another, you and Dores are former schoolmates, and your wife doesn't know anything about it. To me that's strange."

"Yeah, it's strange to me too," Abinasir said, interrupting the discussion. He was bringing Binda the first list of the tenants who had been questioned.

Binda was satisfied with the teamwork he had drilled into his men. He removed the tennis ball with the S.S. initials on it and tossed it twice into the air.

Verga, sitting on a chair, no longer knew where to look and what to answer. He was losing his concentration. He twisted his wristwatch round and round.

"O.K. O.K. Dores and I were together when we were teenagers. And when we met up again we sort of took up where . . . well, you get it, don't you? I don't see the need to say anything to my wife. Do you tell your wives everything you do?"

"But now Dores can't be found. Do you know where she went, or don't you?"

"No."

Binda sighed, got up from his chair and, in a theatrical way, went to look directly into his eyes. Verga held his gaze until he heard Binda whisper, "You don't know us, young man. Do you know what we're going to do now? We're going to tell your wife that you were seeing Dores, and then we'll question your neighbours, someone may have seen you two in her Fiat. Maybe even last night. In the meantime you can call your lawyer if you want."

"I don't have anything to hide, please . . . we're all men here. I gave her the washing machine as a present, she never had a lira, but there's nothing else to it."

Binda decided to call the suspect's bluff, to make him even more nervous. He came up closer and shook his head. "Phone your lawyer, maybe that's your best bet. Here in her house we've found pregnancy test results that show she's expecting a child."

"So you got her pregnant, eh?" Abdinasir said, just a few centimetres from the increasingly grey and drawn face of the suspect.

"I swear I knew nothing, and you can be certain I'm not the father. May I smoke?"

"Sure."

The cigarette brand matched the one found by Cortellezzi in the girl's Fiat 128. It was a widely available brand. Binda held out an ashtray. He would collect the butt afterwards.

When he had smoked half the cigarette, Verga spoke again. "Now I understand why Dores was so strange yesterday, more than usual. We even argued in her car, I slapped her a couple of times, but I swear I don't know where she is. Maybe she's gone to have an abortion, but she didn't say a thing to me about it, maresciallo, nothing at all."

"What about Pallina?"

"I don't know a thing about Pallina, I hadn't seen him in days. I only heard a short while ago that he'd been killed, he was a poor sod that guy . . ."

"And that knife next to the sink? You used that. If the wounds match up . . ."

"Heavens no!" Gino Verga screamed, he jumped up from the chair and threw his cigarette in the sink and yelled "no" again.

In the silence that filled the one-room apartment, he exclaimed, "Don't tell me that Dores killed Pallina."

He turned left and then right, ran his hands through his hair. "Something must have happened here, she lost her head, killed Pallina and then fled."

The carabinieri looked at one another, then Cortellezzi burst out laughing. "Please excuse me, gentlemen, forgive my behaviour, it's inappropriate."

"What's got into you?" Binda scolded him.

"Please forgive me, I'll explain later, really. But can I just explain to this . . . fool, yes, that's the best word for him, exactly what is now going to occur while he calls his lawyer? Since he's the little prince of the squatters here we're going to operate according to his own rules, we're going to break down all the doors. We're going to go into every apartment, empty or occupied, and we're going to find Dores."

"There are still nine of them left to go, I counted."

"We're waiting for authorization from the judge, but at this point, who gives a damn? Isn't that right, maresciallo?"

"Precisely, who gives a damn?" Vicebrigadiere Abdinasir said, standing to attention as though he were volunteering for a dangerous mission on the front line.

Cortellezzi raised his voice, "You'll get twenty years for murder for sure. Which could become life if we add kidnapping to the charge, or if you don't help us, or if you invent stories. If you collaborate there might be some leniency for extenuating circumstances. All of her clothes are here: sweaters, pants, underwear and three pairs of shoes ... did she flee naked? I doubt it. And do you know who they saw running from the scene of Pallina's murder? A thin guy dressed in pink. And do you know who this reminds me of?"

"I was at home."

Binda spoke directly to the suspect, "I'll pretend I didn't hear your lies." Verga began to protest, but Binda cut in with a troubling explanation. "A lot of criminals think they've made a clean escape because they don't realize that they're like the guy who falls from a skyscraper and says to himself, 'twentieth floor and I'm still alive, eighteenth floor and I'm still alive, twelfth floor and I'm still alive, third floor and I'm still alive.' Tell us what really happened, my colleague was right to accuse you."

"May I call my lawyer?"

"Sure, go right ahead."

Verga knew the number off by heart and after calling he returned to his seat and lit another cigarette.

They let him smoke without speaking until the sound of an axe cutting into a door set Verga's lip to trembling again. "Listen, I know it's illegal, but let's say that I am the head of the squatters and you're splitting the doors of these apartments, how am I supposed to keep track of who comes in now? You must know that there are hundreds of families just waiting for an opportunity to occupy places."

"Quit talking shit, you fool. How long do you think it's going to take us to find Dores?" Pertusaro looked at Verga crossly.

"You're on the wrong track, lads. Even if she were behind one of those doors, why on earth would I have put her there?"

"Help us understand, Verga, we won't write a word of the statement until your lawyer is here, but," Binda suggested, "tell us what you know, tell us the truth and not your lies because your situation is becoming more and more complicated by the minute. You know that your squatting racket is a serious crime if proven in a court and we're here gathering evidence."

The man in pyjamas studied Binda, breathed in deeply a couple of times, but said nothing. He jumped at the sound of another door splintering.

"I'd been drinking," he said, and then continued quietly, "We weren't in the car, we were here in this apartment. She was

nervous and didn't want to take her clothes off. She kept looking at the door as though she were expecting someone, maybe
another man. I insisted, but she wasn't having any of it and so I
lost my head and I struck her twice, maybe even kicked her. I
was wrong I know, but I swear I left her there, on that couch
and I went home. That's what happened."

"And Pallina?"

"We ran into one another on the stairs, usually I go up to
the third floor and walk the entire balcony so my wife doesn't
see me. He was crying like he does when he's acting crazy.
Maybe he'd spied on us and wanted to know how Dores was.
But what could I do?"

"You didn't kill him?"

"No, I'm no saint, but I'm certainly not a killer."

"Maybe Pallina went to see Palmira, like he did with the
orthodontist," Binda said, taking the tennis ball with the S.S.
initials from his pocket and lobbing it at Verga's head.

The man caught the ball in one hand and threw it back to
the maresciallo, a sneer on his face. "Palmira doesn't care if I
see other women as long as I come back to her. And Pallina
was a bit nuts, but he wasn't an idiot. He was standing there
with the tennis racket in his hand and I let him go on his way,"
Verga told the doubtful carabinieri.

"Where did Dores end up with all these comings and
goings?"

"I don't know, I can't explain it. Is she really pregnant?
I can't believe it, I'm so careful. I wasn't born yesterday."

"Call Dores' grandmother, I want Verga to repeat this stuff in front of her," Binda said without answering him.

Verga was staring at Binda's moustache, at the wrinkles around his eyes, at his hands, but avoided his gaze.

"Let's take him in: he'll end up being the murderer," Cortellezzi said, but even he did not believe this. All their efforts risked going down the drain. If they couldn't find Dores how would they be able to arrest Gino Verga?

Until then the various stairways had filtered the sounds of voices, of families beginning their day: toilets flushing, coffee-makers sputtering, and washing machines, pots and pans, but now a silence had fallen as the carabinieri began knocking down the last doors.

Affaticati entered the apartment followed by Astrid and Dores' grandmother on her arm. It was then that Binda's mind alighted upon a detail that had eluded him earlier and had escaped his men as well. He took Pallina's tennis ball in his hand again and tossed it a few times into the air and unexpectedly threw it right at Astrid. The woman didn't attempt to catch the ball or to dodge it. Smiling, she said, "what are you up to, maresciallo, playing ball at your age?"

Binda was smiling too and drew closer to her. "Do you know that if it hadn't been for our playboy Affaticati you might have got away with it?"

Affaticati looked astonished. Astrid's mouth, too, was open in surprise.

"I swear I don't know where you're trying to go with this."

"Women as beautiful as you can be good actresses, but it's very difficult to hide physical pain. Your right arm is sore, isn't it? What do you mean it's not? Come on, come on . . ."

Astrid instinctively took a step backwards, but Binda was quicker. And suddenly, as though he wished to strip her clothes off by force, he threw open the front of the motorcycle jacket she had been wearing.

"You bastard, how dare you . . ."

She did not react quickly enough and the open jacket revealed a deep-blue bruise on one arm. A pink T-shirt was visible under the red nightdress.

Affaticati could not believe his eyes. "That shirt is dirty with blood, it was you . . ."

"She wasn't able to change," Binda said to Affaticati, "between running back to her house, and taking Dores with her, all she could do was throw on that nightdress. We were already on the stairs and she had to pretend we'd woken her up. We haven't let her out of our sight since. Go back to her house and let's hope the girl is still alive."

"Oh heavens!" Grandmother Bianca said, kneeling down. She had not understood much of the exchange, but was terrified enough to start praying and throw the fake fur coat Astrid had lent her off her shoulders as though it were burning.

"Quick, someone call an ambulance. May God bless you," Verga had the courage to say, standing up, just as Pertusaro put the handcuffs on Astrid. "My father always said never trust a beautiful woman."

## *Present-day London*

"And you and your friends, Grandpa, were you happy that you saved that woman Dores?"

The wicker armchair tilted backwards. Yes, they had been happy with the way things had turned out.

"As you already may have guessed, not only was Dores saved, but listen to this, Palmer, she married the vicebrigadiere who had fallen in love with her just from seeing her photograph. That man named Arturo, the one I found so irksome. If that's not destiny, eh?"

Binda had not told the entire story, leaving out some details so as not to upset his grandson too much. He was not able to describe the state in which they had found Dores, nor the violence she had suffered. Neither did he recount the lies employed by Astrid as she stood in court. And he couldn't explain the reasons for Cortellezzi's sarcastic laugh to his grandson. "People like Verga or Astrid or even that witch of a caretaker make me think of the policemen you see on T.V. They show up and say, "The knife that killed the victim is that one there," and the assassin becomes depressed and immediately confesses. But in real life, for crying out loud, it's far from easy to find out the truth and get a signed confession . . ."

It did not take them long to discover the motive of the violence. From time to time Astrid would ask Dores to keep small pieces of luggage in her apartment. These contained fashion designs she said. Designs that were too risky to keep in her own place, one could not be too careful, several of her fashion colleagues had been broken into. Industrial espionage, Astrid had told her. Each time she would give Dores fifty thousand lire and the young woman, who wasn't exactly rich, accepted without having the slightest idea of what the luggage contained. Once however, Astrid had given her a suitcase with a faulty lock. Dores, on entering her apartment, had tripped and dropped the suitcase on the ground, where it sprung open revealing what was actually held inside. Not designs of fashionable clothing, but one-kilogramme cakes of Turkish heroin. That was what Astrid was hiding. She was supplying the dealers of Stairway C, as well as the open-air drug market of via Odazio. In her bank account the carabinieri found one hundred and fifty million lire, a far cry from the hardship experienced by the other residents of the housing estate.

Dores told Astrid what she'd discovered and said she was no longer interested in seeing her or her suitcases. Astrid panicked. She wasn't placated by the girl's reassurances that she would never talk. Astrid wanted to be sure she would not. Initially, Astrid had attempted to bribe the girl, but Dores did not want her money. Then she had tried to lure Dores into the business by promising her huge earnings and still the girl was not tempted. At that point Astrid decided to silence her for good. She entered Dores' apartment just after Luigi Verga had left, determined to take action. She wasn't the only one who was alarmed; Pallina had also come downstairs, armed with his tennis racket, after hearing the previous argument between Dores and Verga. He was listening outside the door and burst in when he realized that things were quickly turning nasty. The struggle with Astrid ended when she grabbed the knife and threatened to cut Dores' throat. The girl, in the meantime, had fainted and was lying on the ground. "At that point Pallina had raced downstairs and out onto the street, towards the phone booth. He wanted to call me, to tell me what was happening . . . but there wasn't much anybody could have done for that poor guy."

"What about the neighbours, Grandpa?"

"Don't be surprised, Palmer. No-one heard anything, that's what they told us anyway. But it's clear to me, whoever knew what happened didn't say anything out of fear. Because Astrid, who did actually work in the fashion industry, also had a Mafioso boyfriend serving a life sentence for a variety of murders. As we gathered information on her life, we got the distinct impression that she had already eliminated another woman, perhaps out of jealousy, perhaps for a drug deal gone wrong. But this time she was betrayed by the slowness with which she wrote her name. At first I didn't notice this fact, stupidly I assumed she was barely literate."

"You were fantastic, Grandpa. Father says so all the time. Without you a lot of bad people would still be walking around free, committing crimes. You were the rock where that horrible woman Astrid ran aground and smashed herself to bits."

"She did rather. Twenty-two years in San Vittore prison for murder and ten additional years for drug-dealing is what they gave her."

"Did you celebrate, Grandpa?"

"No, Palmer, I never celebrated once after an arrest. There was so much other work to do I never thought of that. With all the paperwork and documents, it was worse than homework during a summer holiday. That Sunday I was so tired that I stayed home the whole day, spending time with your father who was a great kid and with your grandmother, Rachele, who had made wonderful veal chops in sauce for lunch, *rustin negaa*, you know . . ."

"And was it good?"

"Oh yes, it was delicious, I've even learned how to make it. I'll prepare it for you this Sunday, with potatoes and you'll see what I mean."

And on that final note his grandson had returned, satisfied, to his room.

Binda had not had the courage to tell the child how his Sunday had really gone. Half way through his veal chops he had been summoned to the city outskirts on an emergency, in via Moncucco, by a smirking Notarbartoli. Eight people had been killed in a single night, the worst mass killing in the history of organized crime in Italy. It was a macabre record, higher than

Palermo or Naples, confirming that Milan was a city with a hidden side.

The killings had occurred in a restaurant called La Fogna, "The Sewer", not because of the poor quality of the food, on the contrary, but rather because behind the establishment there was a canal where chemical companies poured all sorts of toxic substances. Michele Prudente, brother of the owner Antonio, had gone to check on things when he saw that his sibling had not returned home. And Binda too had ended up in that killing yard, together with Generale Carlo Alberto Dalla Chiesa. The murderers had not just been content to wipe out the competition, they had also killed the elderly chef, as well as a young woman, who was buried in her wedding dress, not to mention three friends who happened to be there by chance at the wrong moment.

No, it was better if his grandson went to sleep with the idea that, after the evening in Giambellino, Dores' destiny had really and truly changed. The following year she was married to Vicebrigadiere Arturo Abdinasir, the man who had found her by knocking down the door of the broom cupboard where Astrid had hidden her seemingly lifeless body in a rug.

In the end Abdinasir was not nearly as cruel as the words he used. In honour of his chief he named his third child Pietro. "Maresciallo, I swear I'll never be able to thank you enough for transferring me to Carbonara Ticino, life is so much better far away from the chaos of Milan. It's paradise here." This was the standard phrase of the ritual Christmas telephone call he received from the vicebrigadiere.

"No problem, Abdinasir. Helping you get out of Milan was a pleasure for me too."

TRANSLATED BY MARK MAHAN

*Wu Ming*

AMERICAN PARMESAN

*My Dear Friend,*

*It is with great Pleasure that I learn from your latest Letter that you are now enjoying full Health. I hope that this may continue, because even without immediately taking up again your long Journeyings, as of old, you may still be very useful to your Country and to Human Kind, if only you would sit down at your Desk to bring together the Knowledge you have acquired and publish the Observations you have made. It is true that many People hold Accounts of old Buildings and Monuments in high Esteem, but at the same Time there are a good Number who find the Kind of Information that you are now able to offer to be of great Interest. For example, I confess that if, during your Tour of Italy, you could find a Recipe for the making of Parmesan Cheese, it would be more pleasing to me than any Ancient Inscription.*

*Here in London recently, yet another Pamphlet has been*

published on the Degeneracy of the American Provinces. The Author repeats the habitual Fabrications about the Animal and Plant Life, but to these he adds a New Particular, maintaining that even the European Culinary Art imported into the Colonies is now become barely edible. I believe the Way of responding to this Provocation consists in reproducing in America the best of European Cooking Skills, introducing not only useful Plants and Animals but also the Traditional Knowledge required, which is not often found in Books, but in the Hands of Qualified Masters.

Further in this Matter, I pray you keep me informed of the Experiments of our Friend Dr Lynch, who as far as I know has not yet succeeded in curdling the Chinese Beans I sent him and producing the Tofu Cheese that I mentioned to you.

And on the matter of Seeds, I would ask you to send me some Rare Examples, to the value of one Guinea, for which Mr Foxcroft will repay you on my Behalf: they are of particular Interest to a London Friend. If I may be of any Assistance to you from here, please do not hesitate to ask.

Your Affectionate Friend,

Reggio Emilia station. Location, the region of Reggio Emilia. Twenty minutes late on a forty-minute journey. I googled the map last night, the meeting's on the outskirts, nevertheless I was counting getting there on foot, going across town to see if it really is Emilia's most nondescript principal city. In that moment, I have no doubts: the sky is a grubby ceiling that leaks water, it's already nine and I'm forced to take a taxi.

"Via Roosevelt, number 28," I tell the taxi driver as I sink back into the seat. I take out my mobile to tell them I'll only be a few minutes late, then realize I've no number to call, having forgotten to ask for it and, even if I did have it, I'd have forgotten to bring it. So I send Federica a text with kisses and a good morning, seeing as I left early, while she and Jacopo were still asleep.

It's a Monday morning rush hour and raining. The traffic's running slowly, the cars like cans of meat on a conveyor belt. I arrive at my destination in the same time that Google Maps said it would take to walk. Let's say I did it so as not to get wet. A thirteen-euro luxury for which I would never be reimbursed.

The Professore's given me the job, "the most able young researcher we have", because an old friend of his is involved. Not enough of a friend to make him shift himself, though, it seems. As usual, he described the business to me in a hurried and absent-minded phone call. When I called him back later for more details, he told me that he knew little about it himself.

"The consortium that protects Parmesan cheese needs a historian specialized in the American Revolution. It's a legal matter."

The head of the law firm handling the case is Ettore Melchiorri. He and the Professore are members of some Rotary Club or other. The appointment is for nine the next day in the consortium's central office.

"I didn't ask for the exact address, but it's definitely in Parma. Someone like you who knows his way about the internet can find it in a couple of seconds."

I did indeed carry out an online search and found that the consortium's headquarters was in Reggio Emilia.

And so here I find myself in a district that's a mixture of small factories, shopping centres and blocks of flats. Telling one from another is a matter of reading the signs more than architecture.

I ring at number 28, go in and the girl at reception shakes my hand.

"This way, Dottor Bonvicini, they're waiting for you."

She accompanies me, her heels sounding like rapid fire along the corridor's gleaming tiles. The walls are hung with publicity posters and still lifes of cheese in pyramid formations.

The girl knocks at a door and politely introduces me. Inside, four men are sitting round a table drinking coffee. Dark or pinstriped suits, shirts white or blue. I thought I'd be the only one without a tie. But I only had one winter suit, tobacco brown, and that had been liberally sprayed with spumante after the last round of degree ceremonies. Strange to say, the more a Ph.D. degree loses its value, the more the relatives come armed with laurel wreaths and Asti Cinzano.

"Please, take a seat, Dottor Bonvicini," says a youthful fifty something. He makes the introductions in so great a hurry I remember only that the guy on his right works like himself for the Consortium, while the two on the left – one about sixty, the other about my age – are Melchiorri, the head of the law firm, and his assistant.

"Avvocato Melchiorri was just telling us that Professore Lolli speaks very highly of you, Dottor Bonvicini."

I force a smile (what else are you supposed to do under these circumstances, say "thank you"?) and sit down with the day's third cup of coffee. On a tray in the centre of the table are some inviting-looking chocolates, but when I bite into one I discover they are cubes of coated Parmesan (or perhaps I should say "in disguise"). It's difficult to know if they're a delicacy for connoisseurs or a cruel initiation rite. Everyone's eyes are pinned on me. I take a deep breath and swallow, trying to forget the experience.

"Well then, I suggest we make a start," the executive says, not wanting to waste any time. "You're already wondering what this is about, aren't you, Dottor Bonvicini? What has an American history scholar got to do with cheese?"

He continues to smile pleasantly. I nod back in silence.

Indeed, Professore Lolli's explanations have been far from clear. I shoot a glance at Avvocato Melchiorri's rather wizened features, but his gaze is still sharp. His young assistant sports an artificial suntan and a tie in a fat Windsor knot.

"In the file we've prepared for you," "Mr Parmesan" continues, "you'll find documentation of a recent legal case in which historical archives have allowed us to make huge steps forward in protecting our product internationally."

I realize only then that I have the classic rough-cloth shopping bag in front of me filled with tiny free gifts and publicity material. I untie a black binder stamped with the consortium's logo and leaf through its wad of pages.

"As you'll be able to read, we've ordered Germany to stop the use of the designation 'Parmesan' for marketing products that don't have our certification. The Germans defended the use by saying that in their language the term's considered generic, synonymous for any hard cheese. Avvocato Melchiorri consulted a philology expert to show that the general use of the term was very recent and had no historical foundation. Did you know that 'Parmesan' even appears in Stevenson's *Treasure Island*?"

He pauses indulgently until I gratify him with a shake of the head and then he continues.

"One of the characters, Dr Livesey, keeps a piece in his snuffbox and since 1897 all German editions of the novel have called this little gem 'Parmesan'. But for every one of those different editions, the expert pointed out German novels published in the same year where other hard cheeses for shaving or grating are mentioned and they never use that designation."

He shows his yellow teeth again.

"Would you ever have said that literature and history could be so important for the food industry?"

Perhaps he again expects me to shake my head. Instead, I reply:

"Well, gastronomy is culture as well."

He hides his amazement, before showing he's happy with what I say.

"Of course. And with these valid reasons, the firm of Melchiorri and partners won the case. The Germans cannot market their hard cheeses under the name of 'Parmesan'."

"Mr Parmesan" beams in the lawyers' direction.

"Please, avvocato, go ahead."

Melchiorri exchanges a glance with his young assistant, who nods slightly and starts to hold forth. Odd this, I was ready to bet he'd never say a word.

"Thanks. Unfortunately, the problem we have now doesn't relate to Germany, but the United States. The legislation that governs European Union countries doesn't apply in America. In the United States, there's a variety of solid cheeses produced in Wisconsin or New York State that can be called 'Parmesan'. However, now an American cheese manufacturer is claiming the right to use the Italian term Parmigiano Reggiano."

He looks me in the eyes, as if to assure himself I'm paying attention and adopts a grave tone.

"As you can imagine, the question is of the utmost importance. The fate of one of our most important national products is at stake."

A newborn's gurgle breaks out in the room. It's my mobile. I retrieve it from the bottom of one of my pockets and frantically switch it off. I hear myself saying some stock phrase about how children will touch everything, when in fact it's obvious that the ringtone in question came into being with adult assistance. In this case, seeing as my mother-in-law is barely able to send a text, there's no doubt about the guilty party's identity: Federica, mother of my little one, who keeps a very serious 1950s ringtone on her phone, but can't resist the temptation of slipping our son's gurgling into my own pockets.

"They want to send me to New York," I moan two hours later on the telephone to Professore Lolli, my train having come to a halt among the piggeries between Rubiera and Modena.

He replies that this is excellent news, a professional opportunity, which is precisely why he suggested it to me.

"So you knew?"

No, but he hoped they would, he says, because it would help someone like me, a nudge in the right direction, an incentive, something that would drag me out of the usual round of archives and libraries. How can you study the American Revolution and not want to go to America?

"It's not that, Professore. I've been to America. It's . . . well, you know, the baby and my partner . . ."

"Oh, come on, Bonvicini, don't keep harping on the same old story. How long will you have to be away?"

"Three days."

"So? Take my advice, go and resolve this matter, it'll be helpful to you, you'll see."

"Er, there's one thing, Professore, no-one there mentioned anything about any money. As you know, I live for my work, but my son does insist on being fed. Can you put in a word with your friend the lawyer?"

He grunted painfully that he would drop a hint about the matter, and then said that I should call him back, seeing as he was in the middle of a viva and had already forgotten what the candidate was talking about.


"I don't know if they'll pay me," I say to Federica, half an hour later, as we come to another stop, this time in the railway wasteland outside Bologna. "I'm not sure they will, but what does it matter?"

It matters that Federica works in a library. She has fixed hours and never sees any overtime. Only two kinds of unpaid activity exist for her: hobbies and housework. You can't put the latter off, but the former you can, if someone wants you to. So that if I go to America without getting paid, it's not real work. I'm only doing it for fun, instead of looking after my family.

"I'm going as a favour to Professore Lolli, it's a matter of research, I can hardly say no to him."

Oh, but I had, several times before. I didn't have to clock in and clock off in my work; I could organize it as I wished. If I've no time to do the shopping one afternoon, it's my fault because I'm not organized. Or perhaps because I want to do something else. As in this case.

And Federica's not totally wrong.

This thing about the Parmesan really intrigues me.

I try to feign a lack of interest at the same time as I explain what it's about.

"An American cheese manufacturer says that they have every right to make our Parmigiano Reggiano. Several autograph letters of Benjamin Franklin have come to light where he talks about a cheese factory in New Jersey. I have to check if they're authentic and what they say. Millions of euros are at stake."

"And what about you? How many millions of pats on the back do you get?"

In spite of the Trenitalia railway network, I'm home by midday. Federica's at work until two, Jacopo's in his grandmother's care. The arrangement is she'll stay until I get back and, in any case, no longer than one o'clock. If I'm careful, I can squeeze in an extra hour's work.

I turn the keys in the lock without making a sound, as I did when I was twenty and staggered home drunk in the middle of the night.

I take my shoes off in the hall and proceed stealthily.

In the kitchen, my mother-in-law's going through all the animals that deserve a taste of banana.

"Let's give a piece to the gorilla, and a piece to the camel. What about the lion? Has the lion been a good boy?"

I slip silently into the bedroom where with some effort I'd managed to squeeze a small desk. The room I was used to calling my study had gone to Jacopo five months earlier in exchange for a quieter night.

I switch the computer on. I want to see if the internet has anything to say about American Parmesan. I had skimmed through the dossier on the train and gone over the young lawyer's words in my mind. Unlike the consortium's executive, he had never smiled. A serious guy, playing the part. On the other hand, I had to be grateful to him to have spared me all the sweet-talking crap.

"Blue Cheese Inc. is a huge cheese manufacturer. The owners say they've acquired a collection of some autograph letters of Benjamin Franklin from an antique book collector, who found the letters sewn into the binding of an old tome and sold them on to them for a small fortune. Good business for the collector, a bad business for us. According to the Blue Cheese lawyers, the letters contain proof that about two hundred years ago in New Jersey there was a dairy producing Parmigiano Reggiano. On the basis of this historical precedent, the Americans are claiming the use of the name as it appears in the letters. In Italian."

When he'd finished, I had difficulty holding back a smile.

Benjamin Franklin had been the subject of my thesis.

I'd studied his political ideas, but I also knew that he was enthusiastic about cooking and agriculture, and as a young man had been a vegetarian and studied the medicinal properties of rhubarb. For a couple of years I'd been looking at his correspondence with Cesare Beccaria – "so I won't have to leave Italy", as I'd promised Federica. I knew the letters between them off by heart and there was certainly no mention of Parmesan cheese. I wonder what will come up if I do a Google search under "Franklin + parmesan".

I scan the results. The first item is an Italian restaurant on Franklin Avenue in San Francisco. The second is a catalogue for a delicatessen in North Franklin, Connecticut. The third is more interesting. It's an article on "Benjamin Franklin and Food". I do a word search in the article for "Parmesan" and find it mentions a recipe that appeared in *Lloyd's Evening Post*, 23 December, 1773, under the heading "Method for making Parmesan cheese, as observed by Dr Leith and communicated by him to B. Franklin". The only quotation cited would be enough to spark off a bloody internecine war: "At this time, Parmesan is not made in the Parma region, but is a typical product of the State of Milan, the most prized coming from the Lodi area." Perhaps with a statement like that, the Lodi province could claim the name of Parmesan for its less noble Grana Padano cheese. But Franklin? The fact that he might have had a recipe in his hands meant nothing.

I try to investigate further, but find nothing useful.

It's ten to one.

I go back and put my shoes on and I arrive home just in time.

Two days later I'm on a plane to New York together with Massimo Ardito, the young lawyer who'd laid the case out and was taking it up for the Melchiorri firm. At least my flight was paid for and even the hotel. The food, I wasn't so sure. Money for my trouble? Forget it. Besides, I had a cheque for my research from the University . . . I couldn't possibly want two salaries at once, could I?

We fly over France at cruising speed and my travelling companion's just finished having a sleep in the place next to me. He'd dozed off as soon as he was in his seat; perhaps it's his way of fighting off the fear of take-off. He sees I'm reading, so he tries flicking through the airline's in-flight magazine, but grows bored, looks out of the window and sees nothing but clouds, shoots a glance at the female flight attendant and is disappointed. I'd already picked up the kind of information you exchange in polite conversation while we were waiting to embark. He's thirty-four, two years older than me, has no children, didn't earn enough, was a Juventus supporter, had only been to America once before on holiday in Miami; he specialized in international private law, patents and trademarks in particular, and I could call him Max. He was hoping to become a partner in the Melchiorri firm within a few years.

I decide to make the first move to clear up a point that was still troubling me.

"This business of the designation ... it's still not crystal clear to me."

He turns to me with a bored look, sprawling out in the seat as far as he can.

"I mean, why can they produce a wine in America and call it a Cabernet while they can't make a cheese and call it 'Parmigiano'?"

He loosens the knot in his tie some more and nods his head as if to say "good point".

"It's because the name Cabernet is generic, it's the name of the grape variety," he says, "You can take that grape anywhere you like, press it and make a Cabernet. 'Parmigiano' on the other hand is a Protected Designation of Origin. It's an internationally recognized trademark."

"I'm sorry, but I can't see how the recipe for making Parmigiano can be patented, or am I wrong?"

He shakes his head.

"The recipe doesn't come into it. It's the environmental factors that count. It's what the cows eat, the air they breathe, the climate. And then the accumulated experience of the cheese-makers."

"O.K., the Neapolitans say that the secret of their pizza is the water of Naples, and it's possibly even true, but the word 'pizza' is used the world over. It's like 'espresso' coffee, isn't it?"

He nods more energetically.

"Exactly. But in order to be clever you have to patent the

whole thing. Doesn't it piss you off that the largest 'cappuccino' franchise is an American chain?"

I think for a moment.

"If it's any good, I'll drink it," I say, then pull a face to show my disgust, "But I've tried what they call 'cappuccino' and it's revolting."

"The only thing they make well is hamburgers," Max says tartly.

"Yes, and they call them that because the name comes from Hamburg in Germany." I continue, "Is the name or the label so important? I mean, let's take, say, panettone."

"Panettone, our seasonal Christmas cake?"

"Yeah. It's made to a traditional recipe, just like Parmesan cheese, but anyone can make it and the consumer can decide if they want the store variety that costs two euros or the specialist baker's that costs ten. Shouldn't it be supply and demand that rules the market?"

He pulls a face.

"What world are you living in, cloud cuckoo land? The free market doesn't exist. It's a utopian concept, like communism. It's not the quality of a thing that sells it, but the marketing. And the Americans have marketing down to a fine art, investing sums in it with so many noughts you'd go grey counting them all. It's already pretty damaging to us that they can call their shitty cheese 'Parmesan'. If they could sell it as 'Parmigiano', you'd even be able to find it in the South Pole. But it's Italian, it's ours, we bloody invented it. Let them stick to Coca-Cola and hot dogs."

"I can't understand whether it's a question of economics or national pride."

"It's both, of course," he says, stealing a glance at me. "Don't tell me you're one of those who doesn't support Italy in a World Cup."

I keep quiet and have a flashback to June 2006. Italy is playing Australia in Kaiserslautern for a place in the World Cup quarter-finals. It's the ninety-fourth minute, nil nil, and clear that if it goes to extra time the big lads in yellow jerseys will make mincemeat of our big babies in blue strip, panting like old men. I'm watching the match more or less on tiptoe with a few friends, drinking Brisbane XXXX beer. I've bought a real wooden boomerang for the occasion and am holding it in both hands above my head as a propitiatory gesture. Then Grosso comes into the penalty area in slow motion, gets the Australian defender to tackle him and dives headlong to the ground. Yes, that good old Italian sporting spirit . . . The referee gives a penalty, Totti drives it into the net and Italy's through to the quarter-finals and we end up getting plastered so as not to hear the celebrating crowds filling the streets.

"Anyway, I make my own panettone at home, with live yeast. It takes three days, but there's no comparison in terms of flavour."

Max looks at me as if I were an alien from Outer Space.

"You spend three days making panettone?"

"It's like playing with a chemistry set, except you can eat the end product instead of it exploding."

He shrugs.

"I'm hopeless in the kitchen. The best I can do is a bowl of spaghetti and a steak. It's a good job my girlfriend comes round and cooks for me most evenings."

"You don't live together?"

"No, she likes her independence, she lives with a friend of hers. And then, I like it too . . ." he pulls a face. "Well, being able to burp and fart freely, you know? And it's only until we have a kid . . . Are you married?"

"No, but I live with my partner. We've a son, six months old."

The steward interrupts us to serve lunch.

Max looks at the contents of the plastic tray without touching them and asks if they could bring him a whisky.


J.F.K. Airport, New York. Seeing as I've been here before, Max leaves it up to me to lead us to the taxis. The hotel is near Madison Square Gardens. I give the address to the driver and relax in the back seat. In actual fact, I know New York very little. When I was doing research for my thesis I went to Boston and Philadelphia. It was only a few years ago and it seems an eternity: Jacopo wasn't even in the pipeline. Since his birth I've never been as far away from him as this and it gives me a slight feeling of anxiety that I try to drive away by fixing my attention on my travelling companion. Max is looking out of the windows at the lights of Queens. He seems on edge, as if some tension inside is preventing him from relaxing. He's certainly not a talkative guy.

"You tired?" I ask.

"A little. But anyway we've plenty of time to settle into the hotel and get over the jet lag."

"What time's the meeting tomorrow morning?"

"At ten."

The hotel is pretty characterless. We put our bags in the rooms and go down to the restaurant on the ground floor. Max points to the "Parmesan with ham" on the menu ("Can you imagine it? An insipid imitation of our cheese with the ham they use for making toasted sandwiches. And just think, if they win the case, they could put 'Parmigiano Reggiano' instead, and perhaps even Parma ham as well, why not?") Dinner over, we each go off to our rooms and wait for sleep to overtake us. I send a text to Federica to say the flight went well, that I'm safe and sound under the bedclothes. The reply comes back immediately, although it must be dawn in Italy, and its contents warm my heart with the memory of her scents and those of my son. Before dropping off to sleep, I hear Max beyond the dividing wall talking on the phone, probably to his girlfriend in Italy. His voice travels with me as I sink into unconsciousness.

The woman is tall and, without question, natural blonde. It's no dream because I was awake two hours ago, shaved, dressed, then shared a watery and far from comforting coffee with Max and a taxi ride to the law firm of Collins & Haynes on Park Avenue, where the furniture alone amounts to what my apartment's worth and where it's so quiet you could hear a fly sneeze.

No, she's real, in flesh and blood there, with eyes as blue as the logo of the manufacturer she's representing. An athletic figure in a tight-fitting grey suit, high heels, perfect smile, her boobs standing to attention as if they want to burst at any moment from her blouse. She shakes our hands and looks us straight in the eye, memorizing our Christian names, which she'll use for the whole of our discussion. She introduces herself as Eileen Stone, but insists we call her Eileen, without any formal title. She's accompanied by a pale-faced and red-haired male colleague, whose name I immediately forget, distracted as I am by Eileen's shining golden hair and low-cut blouse.

Max's expensive suit and elegant tie easily make me cut a poor figure. As I sit down at the polished wooden table I realize that with my corduroy jacket bought in a shopping centre I really have the shabby intellectual look. But who cares? I'm the historian, the bookworm, the dusty appearance all part of the act.

They ask us if we'd like a coffee or perhaps a drink, but we both refuse. On our way there Max had outlined the game plan. "Rule number one: don't be too friendly, don't accept a drink or anything at the first meeting. Rule number two: don't be stiff, but stick to a professional manner and – rule three – leave the talking to me. Fourth and final one: remember they're the opposition. The bad guys."

The bad guys had also prepared a dossier. Leather-bound, no less.

Eileen has started to speak and I have to concentrate to

follow her English. I'm more used to reading than hearing it and I didn't want to miss anything. "In the dossier you'll find a copy of the original letters and a certificate of authentication signed by Professor Richards of Princeton University." She gives us another gleaming smile. "He's the most important American scholar on Franklin's work."

Well, who could say anything against Richards? I based my whole thesis on his publications. I can barely stop myself from telling Max this, but then I remember the orders I received and keep quiet. Max's eyes are fixed on this Stone lawyer, Eileen, that is, without batting an eyelid. I imagine he's weighing up the opposition, trying perhaps to gather from the inflexion of her voice what eventual weak points his adversary might have. It's difficult for me to tell. She explains that her client, this Blue Cheese Incorporated, already has plans to manufacture the product, and could be in production within a matter of six months. Then she invites us to examine the documents.

I open the folder and there they are: facsimile copies of Benjamin Franklin's letters, rediscovered by a bibliophile blessed by fate. They're only four short texts. Eileen tells us to take our time, there's no hurry, and informs us they've sent off a researcher from Princeton University to carry out another investigation.

Max displays the first smile since I've met him and says that – yes, speaking for me – I'd prefer to examine the material at leisure in the hotel. This information doesn't dent the blonde goddess's cordial manner one millimetre.

"Of course, as you wish. Should we fix a meeting for tomorrow morning, then?"

The deal's done. In case of any eventuality, Eileen leaves us her business card with her mobile number.

We say goodbye. I realize I've followed Max to the letter. I'd said not a word.

As we're taking a taxi back to the hotel, I hear a grumbling through clenched teeth that "the more beddable, the bigger the shits they are."

"Why did you want to go back to the hotel?"

He looks at me askance.

"I don't think you've got it. These people are sharks; they'll eat you alive. If we don't move with leaden feet, they'll leave only a pile of bones. You think I should sit in front of the Virgin of Sorcaya there and do my classwork like a good little boy? We need a bit of strategy, damn it."

"You mean keeping possession of the ball, Italian style . . ."

"It's called taking your time. We'll go up to our rooms now and you can set to work. Then I'll call Melchiorri and we'll see what to do next. In the meantime, we've come to learn one thing: Blue Cheese Inc. doesn't feel it has everything covered. Otherwise it wouldn't have hired a researcher to get more proof about this story.

I nod.

"It means that even the bad guys have a margin of uncertainty."

We get out of the taxi at the hotel. So far Max has paid for everything, because he said he puts everything on the firm's expense account. Well, I certainly wasn't going to object.

As soon as I'm in my room I call Federica and cheer up on hearing her voice. I tell her everything's going well, ask after Jacopo, send a kiss down the line and say we'll see each other the day after tomorrow.

When the call's over I settle myself down at the desk and start to read Professor Richards' report, together with the expert opinions of a Harvard philologist and a palaeographer that knows Franklin's hand better than anyone else. Then I move on to the letters of old Ben himself and copy the "incriminating" passages into my laptop.

*London, 25 March, 1774*

*My Dear Friend,*

*I have read the Report of your Researches with great Delight and in the same Manner I beg you to continue them, because I am certain that the Climate and Nature of the Places are of the greatest Importance in the Production of the Parmesan Cheese, that we have rather stubbornly decided to introduce to America.*

*If, therefore, when you read this, you have still not found a Village in the Boston area most suitable for our Ends, I suggest you make exploration in the Colony of New Jersey. Without wishing to give any credibility to those Denigrators of the New World, it is necessary to say that our Country has a harsher Climate than that of Europe. The Choice of a more Southerly Latitude with respect to the City of Parma could therefore restore some Balance to this Disequilibrium.*

*As in the Area of Origin, the Summers are hot and humid in New Jersey, while the Winters are rather cold and receive snow. The Land is level, fertile, abundant in Water and Clay.*

*Large Cattle Farms are already in existence in this Region and for some time past the Dutch Colonies have introduced and spread the art of cheese making, so much so that the Region's Cheese is highly sought after and the Merchants who come to the City to sell it are called Cheese Wheelers, with a certain Envy over the excellent Business they carry on . . .*

*London, 7 August , 1774*

*. . . Thanks to the Dedication of an Italian Friend, I have managed to acquire, for quite a reasonable Price, thirty-four Head of the red Reggiana cattle. The Number is in effect higher than that we had agreed upon, but the Amount spent to acquire them is half, therefore it seemed wise to disburse the Money freely, given that at least a dozen Cows will not withstand the Rigours of the Voyage.*

*The Herd should be embarked for Philadelphia at the end of Summer . . .*

*Unfortunately, in spite of what we had hoped, our Italian Cheese Maker cannot get to Brunswald before that Time. However, he has drawn up a detailed List of all the Qualities*

*that the different Buildings should have, from the Stalls to the*
*Ageing Rooms, as well as the Implements, such as the large*
*Copper Pans, which should already be in place.*

    *As soon as I receive this List, I will have it delivered to*
*you by Return of Post . . .*

                                 *London, 18 January, 1775*

*My Dear Friend,*
*I received your Letter this Morning with the News that the*
*first Forms of Parmesan have been placed in brine. It is both*
*moving and cruel to think that it is only after many Months*
*that we will know the Results of this historic Experiment.*

    *As regards myself, I think I will leave London well before*
*that Time. Because of the troubles in Massachusetts, my*
*Activities here are ever more unpopular and they are now*
*shamelessly accusing me of being a Sower of Sedition and*
*a Spy . . .*

Through the wall, I hear Max on the telephone. He's arguing with someone, most probably his girlfriend. After four years of living together with a partner I'd developed a certain ear for some of phrases that crop up between a couple.

When I can no longer hear him speaking, I get up and knock on his door.

"Come in."

He's in his shirtsleeves, sitting on the edge of the bed, looking grim.

"Trouble?"

"No, no. The usual grousing with my other half. So, what can you tell me?"

I wave the sheets of paper in my hand.

"They've brought in the big guns. The best academics around."

"Can we ask for additional expert evidence?"

I shrug.

"I'm not sure . . ."

"Oh, come on now," he says, pointing a finger at me. "You're the historian, this is what you're here for. Can't you make an effort?"

"Well, alright. Given we could find someone ready to challenge a man like Richards, it's still his opinion that would count for more. Richards is an authority. Then there's the philologist, the palaeographer . . ." I tell him, letting my arms fall limply to my sides. "Max, I really believe the letters are authentic."

He brushes a hand through his hair and starts to huff.

"O.K., so there's no arguing with that. Have you got any good news?"

I sit down in the armchair next to the bed and rustle the papers with my fingers.

"Well, in the last letter Franklin says the Parmesan's been stored for ageing. But there's nothing more. I mean, what happened to the cheese? Did they really produce any? Did anyone try it?"

Max's spirits seem to revive a little.

"And your point?"

"I think this is the evidence that the Blue Cheese people are looking for in New Brunswald. In order to demonstrate a precedent, a tradition, they have to find out if the experiment was successful or not. You said yourself that environmental factors are crucial for the quality. On the basis of what they have in hand, they can't know if anything even remotely resembling Parmigiano Reggiano was produced down there."

"Excellent, you've discovered their weak point," he says, taking a look at his watch, "I'll call Melchiorri and explain the situation. He has to give us a free hand for more research."

"More research?"

Max takes a few steps around the room. He wants to light a cigarette, but remembers there's no smoking and puts the packet away.

"If Blue Cheese Inc. discovers anything more, we have to know about it straightaway. Or rather, we have to know more than they do. If they manage to prove that two centuries ago they made real Parmesan in this New Brun–shit, the business will turn nasty for us. If our Miss America has an expert in place on this, then we'll have ours."

"Which means me, I take it."

"It's your job, isn't it?"

"My job? I think you're forgetting I'm not being paid. And I have to get back home, I have a baby son and I promised Federica that . . ."

He places himself in front of me with a wicked look.

"Listen to me. Have you any idea what I've passed up waiting to have a case like this in my hands? I've been working for Melchiorri for six years and never a decent court case. I'm sick of kissing backsides. This is an international case and they've sent me. And not just because I'm the one who speaks the best English, you follow me? And you don't think I have any problems at home? My girlfriend's been breaking my balls for two whole days. We were about to go to Sharm el-Sheik. This trip's made the whole thing go tits-up."

He sits down on the edge of the bed again. For the first time I see a genuine expression on his face.

"Shit, I mean we're talking about the fate of one of the most famous Italian brands throughout the whole world. Do you want these people here to snatch it away from under your very nose? That shit of a lawyer said they could start production in six months' time. Now it's down to us to stop them."

I think for a moment. Perhaps I can attempt to broker something.

"Let me do a little research on the internet, O.K.? We don't even know where New Brunswald is."

"It's in New Jersey," he says, pointing his finger towards the window. "On the other side of the river, if I'm not mistaken. Tomorrow we'll hire a car. I'm going to phone Italy right now and speak to Melchiorri. Then I'm going to call Eileen Blue Eyes and cancel tomorrow's meeting."

"Why?"

"To put a bit of pressure on her. She thought we'd read the

letters and go back to Italy empty-handed, dragging our balls on the ground. Better to let her know that things are not going to go as she planned."

He's already fiddling with his mobile. I get up and go back to my room, pretty upset. I also have a call to make. To Federica. And how do I explain this to her?

How times change. When I was eighteen months old, my father was offered an important promotion. But he would have to work for five years Monday to Friday, six hundred kilometres from home. He would see us only at the weekend, but his salary would be almost double. He and my mother spoke together. On one side of the balance they put the money and his career, on the other their relationship and the effects it could suffer. They chose the money.

Today, if anything like that happened, Federica and I would talk about Jacopo, not about us. And in the end, we would give up on the money. My father brought the money home and had no idea even where the nappies were. My seven days away from home, however, are already a challenge to our family organization.

"Here we are," Max announces at the wheel of the hire car.

The name of New Brunswald dominates the totem pole of road signs planted in the traffic island on the state highway.

Immediately below it are two smaller tourist signs. The first welcomes visitors to one of the historic centres of the American

Revolution. The other is gleaming new, and looks as if it had been put up the night before: *Welcome to New Brunswald, the home of American Parmigiano.*

On the internet I discovered that New Brunswald stands on the old King's Highway, the colonial route that Washington's army followed on its retreat to Philadelphia after the loss of New York. The little town even had a local hero, Albert Rice, who sacrificed himself in order to delay the British advance while the rebel army put itself safely on the far shore of Ockervil Creek.

We cross an endless residential area, where the same blocks of housing seem to repeat themselves endlessly and even the hedge height looks to be fixed by local statute. Fortunately the car's satnav isn't playing any games and points us directly to the town's civic centre, where the public library stands with its small local history archive.

Just a little further ahead, a crossroads with traffic lights marks the border between the lines of houses and the handful of six-storey blocks in shades of grey.

We park the car outside a shop with three windows selling household goods. The first window is full of graters of every kind: simple, electric, with a handle, cubical, pyramidal. In another is a display of knives for cutting hard cheese, those with a blade shaped like the spades on a deck of cards, all embedded in a log of wood. On the shaft, several have Benjamin Franklin's signature in rustic pokerwork. Other larger ones have a medallion set into the handle. In the centre, a mountain stands out over a conifer wood. I take a closer look: the mountain's a slice of Parmesan with the appearance of Monviso, better known throughout the world as the Paramount Pictures logo. Around it are the words: *American Parmigiano – New Brunswald – Since 1775*.

Max stops outside the window.

"Can you hear that noise?" he murmurs as I come up.

"What noise?"

"My knackers getting in a twist. This is going from bad to worse."

He skips the bowls for grated cheese in the third window and homes in on two young girls sitting at a folding table under a pop-up gazebo.

I follow him.

Before he can open his mouth, one of the girls waves a pen in his face.

"Would you guys sign our petition? We're asking the government to add New Brunswald to the sites of national gastronomic interest."

I glance at the picture on her T-shirt: the Monviso of Parmesan is there again.

I smile and drag Max away before he can bring charges against the whole of New Jersey.

Directly opposite the library stands a colonial-style building dwarfed by an office block and a multiplex cinema. At first sight you'd say it was an old inn, but it's been so restored it's difficult to say with any certainty whether it was built three years ago or three hundred.

A brass plate by the door says "Albert Rice Museum". Above the architrave, an inscription on the white wall declares that George Washington, the first President of the United States of America, spent the night there on 12 December, 1776. A party of schoolchildren, led by their teacher, is about to enter. The waiting kids sing the national anthem waving tiny flags, as I happened to see once in Cuba for a public appearance by Fidel Castro.

"Should we go and have a look?" I suggest to my companion. "Perhaps it might be interesting."

Max looks at me with the same pained expression as that morning.

"It must be one of those crappy shows where actors dress up like idiots to recreate battles of the past." He looks at his watch. "There's just time to call Italy. Things are worse than I thought here."

I leave him fussing with his mobile. Ten minutes later I'm in the courtyard of the ancient inn where Washington once slept and find myself watching the strenuous resistance of Albert Rice, alone against the British army.

The teachers have a job holding back the cheers of their pupils as the hero of New Brunswald barricades himself at the top of an artificial hill behind a wall of logs and tree trunks. Perhaps they don't know his days are numbered. Or perhaps they do, but think that with a little enthusiasm they can change the course of History.

The audience's passion becomes uncontrollable when, at

the end of his ammunition, old Albert makes his barricade collapse and fall down on the attacking redcoats. The logs roll madly down and, judging by the British soldiers' faces, one or two are really hurt. Nurses go to help the injured while the main body of troops hurl themselves after Albert Rice.

When they come back onto the stage, the hero's in chains. Behind their backs, a haystack is burning.

The schoolchildren are booing and hissing, launching paper balls and paper aeroplanes. As the British line up the firing squad, it occurs to me that right in the middle of these heroic events, the wheels of Parmesan that Franklin desired were sleeping soundly in a cheese factory somewhere in the area. It takes two years of ageing to obtain the King of Cheeses. If the experiment began at the start of 1775, as the letters bore witness, then by December 1776 the ageing process was not yet over.

I get up and go to the lobby of the small museum. Inside it, there is a display set out in a single room. Various panels illustrate the history of the Revolution for schoolchildren and a picture in Disney style shows Washington's historic overnight stay in the little town. On the other wall hang several "designer aged" pictures showing how Brunswald might have looked in the last quarter of the eighteenth century and a very modern illustration of Albert Rice's heroic sacrifice, a totally hypothetical bust of whom stands by itself in one corner of the room. The episode concludes with the British setting fire to the town. Without a doubt, this is the most interesting detail for our investigation.

There are even some antique objects. In a glass case running along the wall you can admire the musket with which the local hero intrepidly resisted the redcoats; a neckerchief that, according to the label, he was wearing when he was shot; and several tools belonging to him: a pair of blacksmith's tongs, a hatchet, a leather sheath containing a small hammer and an iron needle, a snuff box and a bone-handled razor carved with floral designs.

O.K., I decide that's enough. I had better go and find Max.

I find him near the car talking on his mobile again. This time in English. I pick up a few words and a clear "See you later. Bye."

"Who are you going to see later?"

"Oh, there you are . . ."

He gives me a distracted look as he slips the phone into his pocket.

"Yes, new orders. I'm going back to New York tonight."

"To do what?"

"Have dinner with Stone, the Blue Cheese lawyer."

"But didn't you say no friendly relations with the bad guys?"

He brushes my comment away with a wave of his hand.

"Just pre-game strategy. Now things have changed. I didn't expect this," he said, pointing to everything around us. "It's clear that Blue Cheese has done a pre-emptive strike and playing dirty. It's spread the word and now look at the T-shirts, the petition, the signs everywhere . . . these hicks here think they've already secured a paragraph in the East Coast tourist guides."

"Well, they won't get very far with their local hero . . ."

"I don't care where they're going. But we have to get things clear with the opposing legal team. They shouldn't start counting their chickens before they're hatched."

"So you're going to ruffle Eileen's feathers for her?"

He sighs.

"A little of the carrot and a little of the big stick, I think," he says, while studying his reflection in a window and patting his hair. "But this also depends on what you can find out. Off you go to work: the library's at the end of the street."

He leaves me the address of the hotel and goes back in the car.

There are two of us consulting the historical archive for the years 1775-76. The other man is dark, wears spectacles and is more or less my age. When our eyes meet, he smiles and I reckon that I might as well put my cards on the table. I introduce myself and he replies in Italian, which leaves me speechless.

"You're Carlo Bonvicini, of course. Pleased to meet you. I'm Francesco Borghi."

"How did you . . . ?"

"Eileen Stone, the lawyer, called me. She told me you might be coming."

I could have imagined anything rather than discover that

the opposition's historian was Italian. And so instead of consulting the documents, we end up telling each other our life
stories. Francesco left Italy immediately after his doctorate. He
was in London for several years, specializing in Franklin's
English period. As a result, he managed to put a good C.V.
together and got himself noticed, enough to jump across the
pond. Since then he'd done the rounds of different American
universities, wherever they were happy to give him a contract.

"I'm working with Richards now in Princeton."

With Richards no less? The guru of American Revolution
studies? He was only the beacon for all us poor mortal
Americanists.

Francesco laughs at my amazement and plays the whole
thing down.

"It's fine for now, but if they get tired of me they can replace
me whenever they like. I'm used to it by now, I've been doing
the rounds for years. At Brown, Columbia, then Harvard and
now Princeton. They pay well, but you can never stop anywhere."

I'm almost embarrassed to tell him of my measly research
grant from Bologna University. I'd never even attempted to leap
anywhere else. In fact, after research for my doctorate, I'd had
to keep my movements to a minimum, blessing the internet
and Amazon.com.

"I've started a family . . ."

"A family?" Francesco smiles. "I don't even know what it
means. That's a luxury in these parts."

"It's not much better in Italy, but we manage to get by."

A feeling of embarrassment followed that caught us both, as if revealing something of ourselves was putting us face to face with the paradox of the opposing roles fate was dealing us.

Francesco walks with me to the archive. The shelves of interest to us are full of ring binders. After a few moments I have in my hands a map of Brunswald dated 1775, protected by a plastic laminate. In Italy it would have taken me weeks to be able to consult a document of this kind.

"Here you are," Francesco says. "I think this might be useful to you."

I look him in the eye to see if we're following the same track, while Max's words come back to me: "Remember they're the opposition. The bad guys."

"Are you sure about us collaborating?"

"There's not much material to check," Francesco says. "We might as well share it. But perhaps you already have an idea . . ."

I nod. I really can't be diffident with this successful alter ego of mine.

"If the British burned the town down in December 1776 . . ."

". . . Then the cheese factory could have gone up in flames along with a large part of the town . . ." says Francesco, finishing the sentence off for me.

"Well, yes."

I wasn't expecting the opposition to accept my intuitive conclusion so willingly.

Francesco studies the map of the period that lies between us.

"It probably happened exactly like that." He looks up at me with an amused look in his eyes. "But the question is: what happened to the cheese?"

For many parents, the worst nightmare is the newborn child crying out at night. It's normal at the beginning, the little one feels hungry and wants feeding, but once that phase is over, it becomes a total psychological drama. If you calm the baby down, then you are spoiling him (and the bottle at three in the morning becomes a torture). If you don't calm him down, then you don't sleep. We had been fortunate that after three months Jacopo had stopped crying out. Up to then, Federica and I had taken turns to rise like zombies and feed him. It hadn't lasted long, but enough for it to have left its mark on me.

If anyone suddenly wakes me, I immediately think I have to go and prepare the bottle.

Then I check the time to estimate the extent of the damage and see how much sleep I have left.

But here in the hotel I have no alarm clock on the bedside table, my mobile is off and a wristwatch isn't one of my accessories.

There's a knock on the door, I go to open it and when I see Max I wonder if the night has long since passed.

"I thought you were staying the night in New York? What time is it?"

"Depends."

He says this in a vague and pensive manner, which with anyone else you could have taken for a philosophical question, but seeing as it's Massimo Ardito, lawyer, it's more probable that he's referring to the different time zones.

He slips into my room and lets himself slump into the armchair in the corner without so much as a glance in my direction.

I go to pull back the curtains to see what time of night it is.

It's dawn.

Max opens the mini bar door and takes out a shot of Jack Daniel's. From the face he makes as he gulps it down in one go, I'd say that he was over getting plastered and is now at the stage of using alcohol as a homeopathic remedy against a headache.

I'm about to ask him how it went with Eileen Stone, although you could see all too easily the evening had not been a great one, but he catches me on the wrong foot with the first question.

"So, what did you find out?"

I swallow a yawn and point to the notes gleaned from the archive.

"We examined the few written statements, a diary . . ."

"We? We who?"

"Well, me and the historian hired by the bad guys. We joined forces in the name of conscience."

I wait for him to fly off the handle, but instead he lowers his head and massages his face.

"You better tell me the whole story," he says through his fingers.

I sit on the edge of the bed, facing him.

"Washington's army camped at Brunswald the night of December the twelfth 1776 and left at dawn the next day. The British who were following him arrived on the thirteenth and met with resistance from the inhabitants. Well, in reality, it was only one of them, Albert Rice."

"The guy in the museum?"

"He set up a defence on his own against the lot of them. The British shot him. Then in reprisal they requisitioned the livestock and burned the town. But this slowed them down and allowed Washington enough time so they never caught up with him. So, according to the records, the sacrifice of Rice and Brunswald saved the future president's bacon."

He shoots me a sleepy look.

"Is that all?"

"Perhaps you haven't quite understood. New Brunswald rose from the ashes of the old Brunswald. The town was completely burned down. The only buildings that were left were the church and the inn where Washington slept. It means that the cheese factory had to have been destroyed together with the wheels of Parmesan. So no more cheese factory, no more cows and no more cheese. End of story. Blue Cheese has nothing to hold on to."

I keep quiet, waiting for a reaction. I wasn't expecting him to dance for joy, but nor that he would sprawl there looking at me with that face.

"Well done. Question sorted."

"This means we can go home?"

"I should think so."

His lack of enthusiasm is starting to irritate me.

"Don't show your pleasure, will you?"

He sighs.

"I'm not like you are. You bake your own panettone, bathe your little son. You'll go home now and be happy. What do you care?"

"Listen, Max, fuck off, will you? Do you think my ideal's the nice little family of Mulino Bianco biscuit ads? I work, I study, I've even come over here, I work my arse off like you and not even a bonus."

He raises a hand and waves it about in a sign of surrender.

"O.K., O.K., let's leave it."

It's time to change the subject.

"How did it go with Eileen Stone?"

He gives me a bitter smile.

"You know she's a year younger than me? After dinner she invited me back to her house. She lives in a penthouse with a view of Central Park. A little place that I could only get with a fifty-year mortgage. I made myself at home, looked at her and realized that those fifty years were the real difference between us. The amount of time it would take me to get where she was: same salary, same career, same hours in the gym."

"An interesting hypothesis."

"It's not a hypothesis. It's how I felt last night. A drooling eighty-year-old. There she was, inviting me in. She would have had it off with me and no messing. A young handsome genuine Italian lawyer, full of repressed vitality."

"And then?"

"I left. I saw myself in the mirror and it was pitiful."

It must have been the lack of sleep, the time difference and what Max said that made me think of Francesco and his post at Princeton, and I begin to feel less happy with the result. I could hate him for that.

"Listen, you said yourself that this case could turn your career around. We have the documentation now, the historical proof. You can wrap this case up. We can go home in triumph."

He gets up slowly and nods. But he pauses on the threshold as he reaches the door.

"You know, in the end she had a defect as well. Her breath smelled."

He says it in the tones of one of Perry Mason's punchlines and manages to extract a smile from me.

Federica had come to meet us at the airport. The sliding doors opened like a stage curtain and there she was, Jacopo in her arms, pointing a finger at me with one of her expressions, 90 per cent joy, 10 per cent reproachfulness. I wasn't sure the little monster would recognize me straightaway: at six months old, a week is a long time. As soon as he saw me coming towards him, however, he leaned forwards and stretched out his arms and soppy old me thought of Francesco, Princeton, Professor Richards, and said to myself that at least I'd managed to make one right choice in life.

Max asked us to take him to the office, without stopping by his house. I imagined his girlfriend was waiting for him and perhaps he wanted to avoid any arguments.

In the car he went and sat in the back next to Jacopo strapped in his safety seat and made him laugh the whole way with stupid little games, so much so that Federica asked him if he had any children himself and I thought that, when all was said and done, he could well have been suited to changing nappies.

Before leaving him outside his office I shook his hand.

"Well, goodbye, then. It's been brief, but eventful."

"Yes. I'll see you. Ciao."

I watch him walk up the office block steps and while I'm thinking that I might never see him again, I feel vaguely sorry. In the end, he wasn't unlikeable. Then Federica passes a hand over my eyes to check that I'm not off in a dream.

"What do you say, shall we go home? Your son needs to be fed."


Jet lag. I wander about the house, reply to the backlog of e-mails, lazily surf the internet. My eye falls on the Blue Cheese

Inc. dossier, chucked on the desk overflowing with books and papers. I open it and run through Franklin's letters. The question takes shape a little at a time, until it becomes clear.

The Italian Parmesan went up in flames, but what happened to the cheese-maker from Parma?

I'm rooted to the chair, looking for a point to focus on. The cheese-maker. A man who left here, from Emilia in 1774. If I stop looking at this business as a fight over marketing and get back to my role as a historian, I realize this is the real discovery: the story of a guy who left Parma in search of a most unusual fortune in America armed with only his know-how and a small herd of cows. Who was he? What happened to the Italian who went to New Jersey to teach the Americans the art of making cheese?

It would be an interesting angle for a research paper. Before anything else, I had to get myself better acquainted with the art in question.

I find the consortium's website on the internet and start to click on the titles at random, reading several lines of text here and there: the place of origin, its history, the seal impression, how the cheese is checked . . .

I'm sure I can find some books about regional cheese manufacture. Sleep begins to overtake me. I wonder, how could I not be able to sleep now? I'm about to close the website when a corner photograph at the top of the page attracts my attention.

I feel a wave of shivers as if from a Japanese horror film.

Two small hammers, a huge pin with a ring at one end, a leather sheath.

I swallow, as I read the note that explains the methods of quality control used by the expert cheese-maker during ageing.

The expert also uses several tools, which are: a small hammer for tapping, a fine needle with a screw thread, a sample plug or wedge.

By the method of "tapping", that is, by beating the hammer on the cheese, the expert can make a judgement on the cheese's internal structure: it is, in a manner of speaking, an "auscultation". The needle is used to extract a tiny amount of the maturing curds: the resistance of the cheese to the penetration indicates its consistency, and the sample reveals the aroma and degree of ageing. Other characteristics are seen by a simple visual examination.

Taking a sample is rarely practised and only in the case of uncertain judgement.

A flashback. The New Brunswald Museum. Albert Rice's tools.

A deep breath, I have to stay calm. Very very calm.

Should I wake Federica? No, she'd take it badly and let me know it.

I could phone Professore Lolli. I look at the clock. I look out of the window. It is a matter of a few hours.

I have to stay calm.

A week later I find myself in Livorno's Archivio di Stato with Professor Lolli's blessing ("Excellent idea, of course. If your intuition is borne out, a very original research paper could come of it.")

In the eighteenth century, Livorno was the most natural point of embarkation for those from Emilia wanting to get to America. Filippo Mazzei left from Livorno to go to Virginia to cultivate vines and olives. He was a friend of Thomas Jefferson, as well as Franklin. It could have been Mazzei who actually organized the transatlantic journey for the Reggiana cattle and the Parma cheese-maker.

The Archivio di Stato holds the registers for Grand Ducal Customs of 1633–1799. From one of Franklin's letters I know that the cargo left Italy in the summer of 1774. My plan is pretty rough and ready, no more than looking for the Reggiana reds among the customs papers, discovering which ship they sailed on, and then seeing if a the name of a cheese-maker from Parma appears on the passenger list.

I spend two days running through a series of dates, goods and destinations. At the end of every list there are the signatures of the ecclesiastical authorities, the administrator-general and the port superintendent.

On the second day, I find it.

September sixteenth, 1774.
Name of ship: *Il Re del Mare*.
Destination: Philadelphia.

34 head of cattle, consisting of:

22 cows

4 bulls

8 calves

The property of Signor Carlinghi of the City of Parma,

insured for One Thousand Four Hundred gold florins,

assigned to the custody of Signor Adalberto Rizzi.

It has quite an effect, seeing the object of your researches suddenly leap before your eyes at the same time as your intuition proves to be true.

I again see the actors in the courtyard of the inn where Washington slept.

I see again the barricade of tree trunks and logs that rolls unstoppably towards the redcoats.

Once again I see the British rifles pointing at the man who singlehandedly dared to challenge His Majesty's troops to allow the future president to make his getaway.

I leave the laptop switched on and rush out into the courtyard, under the bewildered researcher's bespectacled look.

I switch on the mobile, not sure who to call first: Professore Lolli or Federica?

Instead, without thinking, I dial Max's number.

"Hello?"

"Max, it's Carlo, Carlo Bonvicini . . ."

"Oh, ciao."

"Ciao, listen, I think I've made an incredible discovery.

You remember the hero of New Brunswald, Albert Rice?"

"You still following up that story?"

"I think he was the cheese-maker from Parma. He was called Adalberto Rizzi. "Albert Rice" – you get it? It can't be by chance. Among the tools that belonged to him in that little museum are those of a cheese-maker. The Americans weren't aware of it because they know nothing about cheeses. Their national hero was an Italian immigrant!"

"Well done. Well, go on making more discoveries. At least this story was of some use to someone."

"I thought you'd be pleased to know. How's the Parmesan case going?"

"No idea. I'm no longer on it."

"You're joking?"

"You'd think so, but in the end the firm's partners keep the juicy bits all for themselves. According to them, I've too little experience."

Another voice fills the background behind Max, the sound of a loud speaker, announcements in different languages.

"Where are you? In an airport?"

"I board for New York in half an hour."

"You're leaving?"

"I'll say."

"And your job?"

"I told them politely to go and play with themselves. I've some money set aside, it'll be enough for me to get by at the start, and then we'll see. It it goes belly-up I'd prefer selling pizza for a dry crust in New York than kissing arses for nothing in that dump of a city."

"And your other half?"

"She wants a child and a husband who'll bathe it. And you know what? I'd even do that. But in a couple of years I'd look back and I'd feel a failure. No, I prefer to leave it all behind me while I still can. I told you, I'm not like you."

"Well, best of luck, Max."

"Oh yeah, may the force be with you, break a leg and all that. If I get settled I'll send you the address. Take care."

The line goes dead.

I feel dazed for a moment.

Then I call Federica, tell her I have dug up gold and will be back home for supper.

As I prepare to set off for the station, it's difficult to contain my thoughts. In the next few weeks I'll have to do more investigation on my man in the Parma archives. Probably I'll have to go back to New Brunswald and hunt for any further possible evidence.

If my intuition's correct an excellent study could come of this. All I have to do is come up with a good title. I could send it to Francesco Borghi at Princeton. They could perhaps publish it in some American academic journal.

After all, you're not obliged to emigrate to spread the word. And, again, there can't only be one way of avoiding the future Italy holds for us.

I go back inside and gather up my things. I decide to walk

a bit to get over the adrenalin rush. The train leaves in an hour and I can allow myself a look at the sea from the ancient pier built by the Medici.

While I watch the sun setting on the Tyrrhenian's gleaming mirror, I find myself again thinking that this is the place from where he left. He certainly couldn't have imagined he'd become the hero of another country.

I smile.

I've found the title for the paper.

*American Parmesan: the story of Adalberto Rizzi, a hero across two continents.*

# *Epilogue*

*Brunswald, Colony of New Jersey,*
*12–13 December, 1776*

Standing in front of the cowshed, Albert Rice spat on the ground between the officer's feet.

"You have no right to take my cows away."

Despite his anger, he pronounced the words as best he could, while the cattle filed out under the eyes of a pair of rebel militiamen. Dorina, Viviana, Lodovica, Madame . . . He had baptized his red cows like women loved on the far side of the ocean. Now those names were departing his life for the second time.

Billy was wandering around the haystacks, looking as lost and as sad as his master. He kept his distance from the officer, after nursing the fierce kick received as he tried to bite the officer's calf. Albert had dragged the dog away by the collar, before a rifle butt could split its skull.

"You'll be recompensed, Mr Rice. We'll make a note of the number of cows and the wheels of cheese. I'll sign you the requisition papers."

"And what'll I do with them?"

"When the war's over you can claim compensation for the goods requisitioned."

Albert swallowed. He tried to find the right words.

"And if you lose the war?"

The rebel officer grinned.

"Well, in that case everyone'll be in trouble and yours certainly won't be the most serious."

Albert's face looked even more gloomy. He heard the lowing of the cattle being taken away. A bull was refusing to budge and it was taking three of them to pull it by the rope they had tied around its horns.

He tried to importune the officer again in his rudimentary English.

"These cows come from Italy. They are priceless. They are needed to make cheese."

"If they're good for making cheese, they're also good for feeding General Washington's soldiers. Last night they had boiled roots for their supper. How do you think they'll drive the British to the sea if they've nothing to eat?"

Albert watched two militiamen rolling away the wheels of cheese through the sleet and loading them onto a cart until it was crammed full.

"Sir, we can't get any more in!" one of the two cried in the officer's direction.

"Very well, that's enough. You can leave the rest inside."

Then he turned to Albert.

"You see, Mr Rice? The Continental Army is less greedy

than you suppose."

He made a sign to the others and gave a salute, raising his hand to the brim of his hat.

"General Washington and Congress thank you for your contribution to the cause. Let's be off!"

Albert stood stock-still as he saw them going down the little hill with his cows and his cheeses.

At the first light of dawn, the Committee of Safety gathered the people of Brunswald together and distributed weapons. The law of the colony forbade the possession of weapons in the home. The only two townsmen who knew anything about them immediately complained: the county was responsible for maintenance of the weapons, and these guns were pieces of rust.

Albert had no way to express himself. The times he had used a firearm could be counted on the fingers of one hand. He had pointed this problem out and asked his farmboys to back him up in order to save the Parmesan from being looted. Unfortunately, their familiarity with rifles was a long way from what he had expected: they barely knew where to pour the powder. At the news the British were coming, they had run to shut themselves in their houses.

So when the redcoats appeared on the horizon at noon, Albert Rice found himself alone in his defence of the cheese.

The most robust building of the whole establishment was the large shed for ageing the cheese. It had a single entrance, no windows, its walls the thickness of its pine logs. A few metres in front of the door, Albert built a wall of Parmesan: five wheels at the bottom, four thick and six high. In the little fortification made at the summit, he arranged the weapons at his disposal: one rifle and his hatchet for chopping wood. He mounted the barricade, knelt behind the top row of cheeses and waited.

When they emerged at the bottom of the slope, Albert began to count them. There were a dozen in all, led by an officer; the main body of the troops had remained in the town. The vivid red of their uniforms stood out against the whiteness of the snow that had fallen during the night. They advanced warily, because what with its cowshed, dairy and dwelling, this farm on the edge of town could have hidden half an army. When they made it to the centre of the yard, they looked about them, unsure what to do next.

Billy began to bark without pause, straining at his rope like something possessed.

"Stop or I fire!" shouted Albert from the top of the barricade, trying to stop the barking. The soldiers pointed their muskets towards the sound of the voice.

"The rebels have already taken away my cows. There's nothing more here. Go away."

"That mountain you're sitting on," replied the captain, pointing his finger, "It looks like cheese."

"Yes, but it's not ready yet. You can't eat it as it is."

"We know you've victualled the rebels. Come down and

surrender your arms. I'll sign a requisition paper for your cheeses," he grinned, "You'll become one of His Majesty's creditors."

Albert felt his rage boiling over. He wanted to shout out to the soldiers sent there from God knows where, that he had nothing to do with the war, he was an Italian, and Dorina, Viviana, Lodovica, Madame and all the others were there for producing the best milk for the best of cheeses, and not to be butchered and given to the rabble for food. Years of work were going up in smoke. He thought again about his voyage from Italy, embarking at Livorno, the crossing, the seasickness, the terror of the beasts when the sea was rough, the arrival, and transporting them all the way to Brunswald. He had survived the Atlantic to make this cheese. And now, if he could, he would survive the war as well.

All this went through the mind of Albert Rice, originally Adalberto Rizzi of Parma, while he aimed his rifle from the peephole between the wheels of cheese.

"I do not want your piece of paper and I will give you nothing at all. You have no right!"

The captain lost patience.

"This is your last warning. Come out and surrender your weapons!"

At that moment, Billy pulled free of the rope that was holding him and leaped forwards. A shot felled him in the middle of the farmyard.

And so now even Billy had left him. Albert thought he had

nothing left but the Parmesan. He took aim. It was the only shot he had: he had had the men of the Committee of Safety load the rifle for him and did not know how to repeat the operation.

He fired.

When the cloud of smoke cleared, the captain was on the ground clutching a shoulder and grinding his teeth. He started shouting hysterically, "Open fire! Open fire!"

The soldiers took cover and fired at the barricade. Slivers of cheese spattered over Albert, crouched behind the wheels of Parmesan.

It did not take the besiegers long to realize he was not returning their fire. But however much they fired, they could not drive him out.

The captain barked his orders, the soldiers came out into the open with fixed bayonets.

It was then that Albert swore in Italian, a curse none of the attackers could understand. He jumped to the ground and inserted his hatchet between the third and fourth layers of cheeses. On the other side of the cheese wall he could hear the voices of the British as they advanced.

He heaved on the lever with all his might until the wall collapsed.

The wheels of Parmesan toppled and began to roll down the snow-covered slope, knocking the soldiers down like skittles, cracking feet, shins and ankles.

"The Great Charge of Parmesan Cheese": that was how

it should be remembered in the annals of history, thought Albert as he came out into the open with his hands in the air.

The captain was bawling louder than ever. He ordered the soldiers to get up again. They obeyed, bruised and hurt, and surrounded Albert, striking him with their rifle butts. Then they tied him up and dragged him in front of the officer.

"You are under arrest for sedition against His Majesty. You will be tried and hanged as a rebel."

Albert spat out a gob of blood and saliva.

"I am not a subject of His Majesty. I am not a rebel. I defend my property against thieves."

The captain clutched his shoulder even more, pale and drawn through the pain and humiliation he had suffered.

"In a short time you will have nothing more to worry about. Corporal Giggs!"

The corporal leaped to his side, still a little unsteady on his feet. He must have a fractured a foot, but gritted his teeth.

"Set fire to these buildings."

"Sir, may I point out that we are very close to the town. A little wind and we risk setting fire to everything."

"Well observed." The captain gave him a nasty look. "Now carry out the order, Corporal."


"Dinner is ready, Your Excellency," said a woman's voice outside the tent.

George Washington completed the sentence he was writing,

then opened the drawer under the table and took out a small wooden box, a brush and a pair of pincers.

Inside the casket lay one of the dentures that Dr Greenwood had made to measure for him. With the pincers he gripped the springs that held the two gold plates together and placed them over his gums. He swept the brush over the teeth, hand carved from hippopotamus ivory, closed the apparatus with his fingers and arranged it under his lips. It pinched like hell and if he relaxed the muscles, his mouth would suddenly shoot open, but he had learned to disguise the occurrence with a feigned yawn.

Before going out, he checked in the small mirror above the writing desk to see that his mouth did not look too deformed.

Outside he was hit by the reflections of light on the snow and the noises of the encampment. He came to the general staff's tent, where he found his officers gathered around a lavish spread laid out on the camp table. Colonel Clancy was waiting to give him his report.

The general sat down and motioned him to speak.

"News has reached us from Brunswald, General. The British have set fire to many buildings and shot a certain Albert Rice, who put up the sole resistance barricaded in his farm.

Washington nodded gravely.

"Our cause is favoured, Colonel. Everywhere there are heroes rising up and ready to defend it with their lives."

The general thought the phrase was a well-turned one. With some modification it could be one of those sayings to bequeath to posterity. He would work on it with a full stomach in the afternoon. He pointed to the plate of meat in the middle of the table.

"It looks to me as if those are beefsteaks, or am I mistaken?"

"Yes, sir," said Clancy, "They come from the red cattle we requisitioned, sir. A manna from heaven for the troops."

Washington gave a pleased nod and noticed the other plate. He stretched out a hand and put a piece of the cheese in his mouth.

His palate responded with pleasure. The flavour was both a sharp tang and mellowness.

"Do try this cheese, gentlemen. I don't believe I've ever tasted anything similar. Does this also come from Brunswald?"

"Yes, General. Unfortunately, we could only bring ten cheeses of a hundred pounds weight."

"Exquisite," Washington observed. "When you have time, Colonel, please discover who produced it."

"I should like to answer you, General. But the register of requisitions was soaked with water as we forded the river."

General Washington chewed again to savour it.

"A pity, truly."

TRANSLATED BY N.S. THOMPSON

*Simona Vinci*

ANOTHER SOLITUDE

*For Valentina Misgur,*
*who knows how to be alone*

*There is another Loneliness*
*That many die without,*
*Not want of friend occasions it,*
*Or circumstances or lot.*

*But nature sometimes, sometimes thought,*
*And whoso it befall*
*Is richer than could be divulged*
*By mortal numeral.*

EMILY DICKINSON

ONCE, ON A SUMMER DAY, IN A PART OF THE WORLD where the sun knew neither dawn nor dusk but always hung high in the sky like a lit lamp, a man filled a sack with provisions and essentials, put it on his sleigh and headed towards the invisible horizon. His wife and three children looked at him without saying a word. They knew well that they had lost him the very moment the idea of going away first flashed across his mind. It was already too late, nothing more could be done: when a man begins to be alone in his own head there is no convincing him to turn back. They saw him go on in the white light that promised snow and more snow, his footsteps leaving no visible tracks on the clear white ice of the fjord, and they knew that they were looking at a phantom, a vision of the past, the echo of something that would never again be real. That man had become a *kivitog*.

In Inuit culture, there is nothing worse than being alone. Solitude is a prison sentence; it anticipates death. You live in community: you eat, sleep, use the toilet, go on walks, fish and hunt surrounded by others. From time to time you get drunk together. Without others, there is no life. Even today, houses in Greenland contain a single big common room with up to ten or twelve people living in it. Adults and children, old people and newborns, all live together: the concept of privacy simply does not exist. In fact, Eskimos believe isolation to be a sign of unhappiness. Bizarrely, it is here in Tasiilaq, in this place literally at the top of the world, where someone who is alone is seen as being irredeemably unhappy, that I am starting to write about solitude. Moreover, I am alone, if not especially unhappy. I have walked the streets of this little village of one thousand nine hundred and three souls in east Greenland for many days now. They have watched me arrive, go shopping at Pilersuisoq, the supermarket on the village's main crossroad, and trudge my way back uphill to the Red House. They watch me sit on the icy fjord next to the fishermen, or on a rock that juts out to the sea where you can get a better view of the icebergs and islands of ice, and now at the lit window of the communal kitchen while I cook myself dinner. I know they are observing me, even if they look timidly away when I meet their gaze and smile. Only the children greet me. Some of them even touch me, grabbing the sleeve of my windbreaker or throwing me a ball. A few little girls risk coming to my house and into my room, to play with mascara and lipstick in front of the mirror, but this only happens when they too are alone, not when the adults are around. Perhaps the adults have told them not to trust people who spend too much time alone because they are unhappy and something is wrong with them. Everyone knows that unhappiness is more contagious than flu. And how can you blame them? Where Nature can be as powerful and unpredictable as it is here in the Arctic, being isolated is a curse and a daily challenge for many settlements, and someone who is alone is fragile. He is at the mercy of the elements, of snow, wind, wild animals, ice, cold and his own fears.

A couple of days ago, at the top of a mountain I reached with the help of a sleigh and a pack of Greenland dogs, huskies with brown eyes and reddish fur, I found a little shack made out of red wood. Four walls, a door and a bed of stripped-wood planks. On the ground there was a metre-thick layer of ice. I asked Tobias, the hunter guide who had brought me there, what purpose the cabin served. "It's a shelter," he replied. "When the weather turns ugly, hunters or explorers take refuge here." On a clear day, you can see the ice caps beyond a fjord and mountain range. But that day we could see nothing, and the horizon was milk-white with a faint blue-grey line. It had started to snow. The sky had become even flatter, the dogs were dozing in the snow and Tobias sat on the sleigh eating his sandwich. The silence surrounding us was absolute. There, standing on a rock at the summit of the Sermilikvejen mountain range, I tried to imagine having to stop here alone and wait out a storm in this little cabin in the middle of nowhere.

It is not only the weather, called *sila* here in Greenland, or meteorological conditions, which can suddenly turn ugly. Internal weather sometimes does that too, and solitude can also be useful then. Animals know that, as do some humans: when cats feel ill, they will look for a hidden and protected place where they can curl up and wait for the bad weather to pass. Old Inuit, when they felt that their time to leave earthly life had come, used to have themselves taken to an isolated place, and stay there alone to wait: death would arrive in the form of a wolf, a bear, or hypothermia. In Nicholas Ray's film "The Savage Innocents", the old mother senses that it is time for her to get out of the way. The winter has been too harsh and the family does not have enough to eat. She is old anyway and the strict law of the Arctic demands that any useless mouth to feed must be got rid of – she "understood that the moment to undertake the long journey had come". So her daughter and son-in-law Inuk, played by Anthony Quinn, accompany her to the place she has already chosen, on the edge of the pack ice, in the silver darkness of the Arctic night: a tiny old Eskimo woman sitting on a sealskin on the snow, her back and shoulders to the camera. It pulls away until she becomes a barely visible dot, soon to be swallowed by nothingness. Solitude will protect her death from the pain of those who loved her.

Quite apart from being a refuge, solitude can also be intoxi-cating, a form of taut, uninterrupted concentration, in which a thought can develop in all its completeness, like a nylon fishing line that unwinds from the frozen surface of the fjord enters a hole in the ice and plummets, sunk by the hook and weight until it reaches the bottom of the ocean without encountering an obstacle.

While the snow grew thick, I looked at the blue line that was fading into a white in which nothing would be distinguishable. I knew it was the *Indlandis*, the immense body of ice that crowns the planet. Jack London and Ludwig Wittgenstein suddenly came to mind.

In 1911 Wittgenstein, a young well-bred Austrian with high aspirations, was already an engineering student when he enrolled at the Faculty of Philosophy at the University of Cambridge. He spent two years studying with the distinguished professor Bertrand Russell, arguing endlessly with him. Russell had this to say about Wittgenstein: "My German threatens to be an infliction, he came back with me after my lecture and argued until dinner time – obstinate and perverse, but I think not stupid." During those years, the young Wittgenstein began his work each morning with hope, and ended it each evening in despair, or so he said. Dying, dying, he was sure he would die before long. He kept saying so, and it was the same tune every day. "I'm dying, dying, I know I am going to die. I can't have more than four years left," he would say. One day, he even convinced himself that he had only two months to live, and there was no way of making him see reason. He needed to concentrate, every fibre of his being stretched out towards that thread of invisible horizon that he had to see at all costs. In so doing, he would find the exact words he needed to reveal it to someone else. So in 1913 Ludwig Wittgenstein, who would later be a philosopher, primary school teacher, gardener and architect, but above all a *human being*, unexpectedly left the Faculty of Philosophy at Cambridge to move to Skjolden in Norway. He would be living on the edge of a fjord, in an isolated wood hut that he built with his own hands. Perhaps there he would be able to complete the work he feared he would never finish. To reach the cabin you had to cross a frozen lake: no-one would make it all the way there to disturb him. He would finally be completely, definitively alone. Professor Russell attempted to dissuade him: "It will be dark," he said. "I hate sunlight," he replied. "It will be lonely." To which he said: "I prostitute my mind talking to intelligent people." "You are mad," the professor told him. Wittgenstein: "God preserve me from sanity." And then he left for Norway. Of that period of isolation, interrupted only by a few visits and a few trips, the philosopher was to write in his notebooks fifteen years later: "Incidentally, when I was in Norway during the year 1913–14 I had some thoughts of my own, or so at least it seems to me now. I mean I have the impression that at that time I brought to life new movements in thinking . . ."[†]

★

[†]    Ludwig Wittgenstein, *Culture and Value*, ed. G.H. von Wright and H. Nyman, trans. P. Winch (Oxford: Basil Blackwell, 1980), 20e.

There is now a wooden plaque decorated with an ornamental motif representing a little house, which has been erected by the lake in the village of Skjolden on the Sognefjord, in the heart of Norway. It states these precise words in three languages, Norwegian, German and English:

> The eminent Austrian philosopher Ludwig Wittgen-stein (1889–1951) owned a hut here in Skjolden from 1914 onwards. The remaining bricks of this hut are visible on the other side of the Eidsvatnet. There, Wittgenstein worked on his manuscripts *Tractatus logico-philosphicus* and *Philosophical Investigations*.

Jack London came to mind because of the log cabin on Henderson Creek in the Canadian Yukon, where he stayed at the end of the nineteenth century on his way to join the Gold Rush. There, when he was barely more than twenty years old, he learned what solitude means in a hostile environment: snow, ice, temperatures that could reach minus forty degrees, isolation. He did not make a fortune in gold, but he did collect observations and material for some of his best books. The theme of solitude runs through all the works of this great American author, from the inner solitude of his alter-ego character Martin Eden, a tenacious sailor who dreams of becoming a prominent author in spite of his humble origins and lack of formal education, to that of the dog Buck in *The Call of the Wild* who, separated from his original owner and tranquil life, is taken to the Great North to work as a sled dog. Buck has a series of adventures that lead him to heed the call of the wild and live with his ancestors, the wolves. Finally, Darrell Standing, protagonist and narrator of *The Star Rover*, a former Professor of Agronomics and self-confessed murderer serving time in San Quentin State Prison, California. Darrell has been subjected to a regime of "solitary confinement", called living death by those who have endured it. And yet, during these five years of "death-in-life", he writes, "I managed to attain freedom such as few men have ever known. Closest-confined of prisoners, not only did I range the world, but I ranged time."[†] The star rover is trapped in the cruellest form of solitude a human being can experience, confined to a dark cell and often strapped inside a straitjacket. Yet he finds a way to escape, to experience a thousand lives in different places and times. How? With strength of mind and an extreme effort of concentration. Because we humans, Standing/London tells us, are not only flesh, flesh that can be imprisoned, tortured and humiliated, we are spirit and spirit is indestructible. The mind is indestructible, and capable of shattering walls, of freeing itself from the heaviest of shackles, of hovering high in the sky even when the body languishes in the dark abyss of a prison, in absolute solitude.

When I type the words "solitude" or "loneliness" in Italian into Google, one of the first results that appears is a social psychology

†    Jack London, *The Star Rover* (New York: Macmillan, 1915), 4.

article on the University of Udine's website, entitled: "How to overcome loneliness and find new friends." There are hundreds of such pages online – thousands, if you extend the search to languages other than Italian. These days we consider solitude a curse from which to seek release at any cost, an ailment of both body and soul that mainly afflicts losers, the insecure, the too young or too old, basically, the weak.

As I browse online through statistics and advice on how to purge this cancer from our lives once and for all, I cannot help but think of Thoreau, of his Walden, of the chapter entitled "Solitude" in *Life in the Woods*, in which he writes: "My nearest neighbor is a mile distant, and no house is visible from any place but the hill-tops within half a mile of my own. I have my horizon bounded by woods all to myself . . . I have, as it were, my own sun and moon and stars, and a little world all to myself." Thoreau was surrounded by Nature, and when immersed in Nature you are never alone. "There can be no very black melancholy to him who lives in the midst of nature and has his senses still. There was never yet such a storm but it was Aeolian music to a healthy and innocent ear." Certainly, being alone in a big city is completely different from being alone in nature. Cities are designed to give an illusion of proximity: houses leaning tightly against each other, blocks of flats like beehives, shops where the radio is always on, the constant drone of music, voices and cars that makes us feel like cogs in a great machine, part of a whole without which we might well feel lost. And yet, no scene better evokes solitude and loneliness than that of a man stretched out on a damp piece of cardboard on the pavement of a big city, while the crowd walks by without even deigning to look. Where does this story take place? It is a story repeated thousands of times a day, in every big city. Even in mine, Bologna, a hospitable city by definition, but now no different from any other metropolis.

It was a late winter evening, Christmas was near, the city's streets were festively lit and everyone was in a hurry, everyone was running, their arms full of packages and parcels containing gifts. I too was running like everyone else, rushing to get home. It was cold and I wanted a steaming hot bath. Beneath the arches on via dei Mille, near the crossroad with via Indipendenza, there was a girl sitting on the steps of a bank building. She was alone. She was writing something on a piece of cardboard and crying. Crying desperately. The tears dripped down her round baby face. But no-one stopped. The mad rush of the world continued although a girl was crying, desperate and alone. Even I walked past her. I did not have the courage to stop, I did not even know why. When I got home I could not stop thinking about this. I thought about it for days on end. Then I accidentally stumbled upon a blog run by the community centre, Asfalto, on via del Porto, and read a piece that told the same story: same place, same time, same girl, same reaction. I left a comment, and that was how I met the group behind Asfalto not long thereafter: one of the few places where the loners of Bologna's streets can meet is this community centre on via del Porto. There is a tele-

vision permanently switched on in one corner of a big room
dotted with small tables and plastic chairs. The centre offers a
shelter, a hot meal, the chance of talking to someone, as well as
an art studio and a computer room for anyone who is interested. Massimiliano is there every afternoon. He encourages all
visitors to be creative, pushing them to write their stories and
thoughts down and to post them on the community centre's
blog, which has become a point of reference for those living
on the streets of Bologna over the past couple of years. Friendships, networks, opportunities, have been born from that blog.
Living on the streets is hard, and although sleeping rough means
always being around people, loneliness is a constant guest. Telling
your story, writing it down, and then rereading it as though
someone else had written it, is perhaps one way to feel less
lonely.

According to a demographic survey conducted in March 2008
by Telefono Amico, nearly four million Italians are sometimes or
always lonely. The data points to Milan as the capital of loneliness. The majority of lonely people are single, aged over
fifty-four, poorly educated and earn low wages. The survey goes
on to reveal that when Italians feel lonely, they do not know to
whom they should turn besides their family, for those who have
one, and that only one in ten Italians would see a therapist. But
even the family can be a lonely place. Living together with
someone, eating at the same table, sharing every single act of
daily life, may not be the perfect antidote to loneliness. There

exists a form of solitude that has less to do with bodies and shared space than with thoughts and emotions. People who live cheek by jowl sometimes survive by becoming impenetrable to each other. I have always thought that living with someone else can make that person lose their otherness, as though they have become an object, a piece of furniture, something functional. It is like that beautiful red armchair you were so excited about buying: two months later, it has become part of the furniture and you barely notice it. You use it, sure, you know it is there, but it no longer occupies a central place in your thoughts. Someone might object that a human being is not an armchair, humans move, talk, breathe, but that does not convince me. I have always needed a certain degree of physical and temporal distance separating me from other people. I find and have found my own pace and rhythm in that space. I regain strength, energy, and desire. Only then does an encounter with the other recover its old charm. When I return from my space of solitude, I know I have something new and fresh to offer, and I can receive the same from someone I meet.

There are two basic kinds of people in this sense, I think: those who associate the word solitude exclusively with unhappiness, distress and failure, and those who breathe a sigh of relief when they hear the word. "Finally!" Or, "if only . . ." I have undoubtedly always belonged to the latter category, and have never been tempted in the other direction. When I was four I had a tepee in my room. I do not remember precisely how it got there and who put it up, only that it was there and it was mine. In it there were toys, provisions and piles of illustrated books – among them, the Brothers Grimm's Fairy Tales, an old edition published by Einaudi that I still have, filled with mummified bread crumbs and pages smeared with jam. I think it was there that I learned how to read. I emerged from that cave one morning at dawn, when the light was pale with winter, and ran to my parents with a Mickey Mouse comic in my hands to announce the discovery: I could read. It happened suddenly, one moment I could not read and the next I could. Of course, my mother must have shown me how to write the letters of the alphabet; she may have had me copy them out on a piece of paper one boring afternoon, repeating the sounds to me and teaching me to associate them with letters. But until that moment, which is the most vivid memory of my early life, I did not realize that I had learned to read. I am convinced that I figured it out on my own. That was how I continued to learn everything in life, taking what I wanted to learn and what I found useful from teachers and masters of all kinds, and then finding my own path and making my way along it as best I could. I never truly relied on anyone, and I loved to play alone. I spent hours hitting a tennis ball against a grainy wall, until I was enrolled at a tennis school and found that there was another child on the other side of the net, and that I was meant to hit the ball to him instead of to my beloved red wall. I did not care much for this novelty, and although I attended the tennis school for years, I preferred to practise against the wall. The challenge, for me, has never been someone else: the challenge is myself. I am the other. There are such people.

The poet Emily Dickinson was thirty when she realized that it was time to close the door, to retire from the world, to hide. It was not that she had not valued and sought out solitude until then, the solitude of reading, writing and contemplating nature, but that year, in 1866, something definitive evidently happened, perhaps something that had been building up for a while: that's enough now, a curtain fell. Behind it, we can still imagine her as though it were today; a girl (because Emily would remain a girl until her death at fifty-five), slender, delicate, dressed in white, a blue shawl, long, dark hair, parted in the middle and tied at the nape. Wherever she went, she left the scent of freshly baked bread, yeast, jasmine and laundry soap in her wake. Her life resembled that of hundreds, even thousands of singles – they used to be called spinsters – who were well off for their time: a big white house looking out onto the main street of the town of Amherst, Massachusetts, in the United States, a beautiful garden, a respectable family with its fair share of strangeness – a fragile, elusive mother and an authoritarian but much loved father. Emily had taken care of everyone for years: of her brother Austin, of her sister Lavinia, of her parents, relatives and friends. She had baked cakes and written notes, sent bouquets of flowers ("Between my Country – and the Others / There is a Sea – / But Flowers – negotiate between us – / As Ministry." No. 905), welcomed guests, loved and been loved, but now she was closing the door. Some called her the "reclusive poet", some thought she was mad. Certainly no-one could imagine that after her death she would become one of the most famous and best-loved poets of all time. Writing is a strange illness. Whether mild or fierce, the disease isolates anyone who catches it in some way, to some degree. It takes extreme concentration, a mental state that resembles meditation, a sort of uncontrolled control. Is that what Emily was doing in her room? She wrote. And lived. The little world that was her home contained news of every other world. As Buddhist monks know, anything, if you know how to look at it, can in fact speak of everything; every place is all places. Emily chose to make herself, an unusual but also very ordinary person, the privileged object of her own study. But nothing in her poems would suggest the terms "auto-biographical", "solipsistic" or "narcissistic". Emily sketched bare, geometrical lines of verse that examine human nature as if by X-ray. She had known and loved the world. Now it was time to be silent, even if she would certainly never stop listening. Her door had never been bricked up or even furnished with a keyhole, it was simply ajar. If we push it open slightly, we can still see her: there is a little light inside the room, the girl dressed in white is putting her pen to paper, she is wrapping a blue shawl around her shoulders, she is opening the window and looking at the garden kissed by the shadow of the evening, the delicate heads of the flowers drooping slightly as though they are asleep. She smiles at the darkness outside. Her pen lies on a piece of paper on the table; the ink is still drying.

*

It was the summer of 1915, and in Greystone, a little fishing village on the east coast of Ireland, there was a boy walking along the tideline alone. He was thin, with narrow blue eyes and big protruding ears, his blonde hair was pushed out of his face and parted to one side. He had a solemn, focused expression: he looked sullen, but flashes of irony passed rapidly through his eyes. He was nine years old and his passion – he would later define it as his "love" – was the rocks and stones that he collected on the beach and took home to keep in the garden, so that the sea would not sweep them away.

If Emily had been able to see this nine-year-old boy who suddenly left the group of friends he had been playing with until then and walked away along the beach by himself, she might have noticed something of herself in him. If they had been children in the same place, at the same time, they might have become friends. He would have given her one of his stones or bones and she could have given him one of her flowers. He would have tried to explain what attracted him to the mineral world, and she what attracted her to the animal or vegetable world. She was fascinated by the process of birth, flowers blooming, buds sprouting bravely and enthusiastically from the ground. He was fascinated by decomposition and death, stones and bones that calcified until they became so fragile they would disintegrate with a single breath. Only he, many years later, could have a character in one of his novels say that he was now going to tell three stories, and that one of them would be the story of a stone. The novel was called *Malone Dies* and the boy who loved stones was Samuel Beckett, one of the greatest playwrights, poets and novelists of the twentieth century and of all time. A need for solitude and the consequent painful sensation of loneliness would haunt him for the rest of his life. "He felt his solitude, sometimes very acutely. But it was a solitude that he also cultivated, obscurely aware that something was happening within him as, eclectically, he accumulated knowledge."[†]

Beckett needed to be alone, but sometimes he could not stand it. At the beginning of the fifties, he used an inheritance from his mother to buy a little house with two rooms in the country- side of Ussy-sur-Marne, in France, about fifty kilometres from Paris. His life now had two halves: there was his work in Paris as a playwright and theatre director with all its obligations, rehearsals, meetings, friendships, and then there was the calm, silence, solitude, concentration of the countryside. There, his writing was interrupted only by walks, bicycle rides, evenings spent listening to the radio, the whisky bottle. "I seem to recuperate something in the silence and solitude", he wrote to a friend.[‡] It was there in Ussy that in the first few weeks of 1958 he wrote *Krapp's Last Tape*, one of his most famous plays, a short monologue in which a haggard old man,

[†]   James Knowlson, *Damned to Fame: The Life of Samuel Beckett* (New York: Simon & Schuster, 1996), 191.

[‡]   Ibid., 353.

alone in his den, recalls the past while listening to his own voice etched over the course of years onto dozens of catalogued tape reels.

Krapp is prophetic: decades before the internet is to appear, he shows us a man alone with technology. Granted, his is primitive compared to what we have at our disposal today: it consists of a reel-to-reel recorder and several tapes. Here is a man locked inside his den listening to his own recorded voice and trying to make sense of the past, to understand his life, to understand why things happened the way they did rather than any other way. This is hardly the same as spending hours chatting to strangers on the internet, you might object. Krapp is alone, alone with this voice of his from the past. There is him and him only, no encounter is possible, no debate. Krapp faces only himself, and prior versions of that self. No, a tape reel is not quite the same thing as the internet, but I cannot help thinking how similar they are. It is true that the friendships born in chat rooms, online forums and the comments section of blogs can often take you from a computer screen onto the street, into a piazza or a room, that they allow us to meet people we would not have encountered in daily life, if only because the soon-to-be close friend, lover even, lives in a city five hundred kilometres away, which we would never otherwise have visited. It is true. Completely true. I have experienced this too. I have made friends who became flesh-and-blood realities, faces with stories to share. And yet, every time I surf, chat or leave a comment on a blog,

I have a sensation that the abyss could open and swallow me up. It could swallow up my time and energies, and suck me into a parallel life from which I would never be able to extricate myself. This has happened before; it happens to people all the time. I think of teenagers shut up in their rooms who discover sex on the internet and become entangled in it. I think of all the people who find a form of release online, a means of escape from monotonous, tiring, too grey lives. How many office workers have I met in chat rooms who, in their lunchtime break or during working hours, keep a pop-up window open in the corner of the screen and send messages, write, play at living a different life or merely a less depressing version of their actual life. Online we have the sensation of always being with people, surrounded by the warmth of typed phrases that light up like L.E.D.s on the screen and pulsate for us, only for us. But all we have to do is switch the computer off and those virtual presences vanish. We are alone again. Perhaps we no longer know what to do with our solitude, we do not know what presences we can fill it with, and we are afraid of it.

Emily Dickinson, Samuel Beckett, but also J.D. Salinger, the author of *The Catcher in the Rye*. He was thought to be dead for many years when he was in fact living in reclusion on his property in Cornish, New Hampshire. He had left New York and retired there in 1953. Only two years after his first book had been published, fame had begun to feel constricting and irritating like a pair of ill-fitting shoes. As the years passed,

Salinger progressively reduced his contact with other people. From 1965 onwards, he never published another line. The artist Pontormo built his studio on top of a tower of sorts. It could only be reached by a ladder that he could draw up from within to shut out the intrusive world. The author Thomas Bernhard was so irked by unannounced visits from family and friends that he sometimes hid his car to make it look as though he were not at home. The poet, writer and songwriter Leonard Cohen, who spent long periods of his life on the remote Greek island of Hydra, retired from 1993 to 1999 to a Zen monastery where he called himself Jikan the Silent. He emerged from it with new songs, with his incomparable voice and the art of always happening to be in the right place at the right time, with a lightness that must have come from years of practice, not just of Zen Buddhism but also of solitude. And the list could go on ad infinitum.

But you do not have to be an artist to want a moment of solitude every now and then. Everyone needs a place to be alone, far from other people's demands and from their scrutiny. Even when it is born of affection and the best of intentions, scrutiny is still scrutiny: it measures, weighs, and passes judgment, even without meaning to. You need a place that is yours, and only yours, because to be alone is to be in your own presence. This could be an extraordinary experience for one person and a nightmare for someone else. One person might need no more than a day or a week, while someone else needs months or years. Only an instant of solitude might fill someone with dismay. I am suspicious of anyone who has never, over the course of a lifetime, desired to be alone: how can you trust someone who does not trust himself? Being afraid of solitude means being afraid of the stranger who hides behind your own face. And as the Greeks warned us, rule number one is to know thyself. If not, how can you truly know anyone else? And if it is true that we know ourselves in connection to other people, in relationships, it is also true that in solitude we sharpen our gaze, we train it in darkness, like a school of apnoea for learning to breathe better.

A 67-year-old man died unexpectedly in a small town in northern Italy. His unanticipated death left an emptiness in the lives of those who loved him, his family and friends. When someone passes away suddenly, unprepared, he leaves doors open and rooms to explore. Places no-one suspected might exist, like a secret cellar full of trunks stuffed with papers that remain to be deciphered. This man, a husband and hardworking father of two, had a secret. His secret was a rented studio apartment in the city centre, not of the city where he lived, but of one a few kilometres away. He was evidently not expecting to die this way or to die this soon, because he had not made a will. His wife and children were stunned to discover the existence of this room, and decided to go there together, even though they trembled as they set out. They were afraid of what they might find, afraid they might uncover something terrible, something ugly, something that would irreversibly alter the memory of the father and husband whom they had loved and trusted for such a long time.

What did it mean, this secret room? Who was this man? Inside the room there was a sofa bed, an old L.P. player, a pile of jazz records, a shelf of detective novels, comic books and crossword magazines. There was a bottle of grappa standing on the table and an ashtray overflowing with cigarette stubs. A drawing pad filled with charcoal sketches was left open, with a half-finished sketch on a right-hand page: the outline of a woman in profile. "But Papa gave up smoking ten years ago! But he only read historical biographies! But he said he couldn't hold a pencil properly anymore!" In the studio's tiny bathroom were brushed-cotton pyjamas and a pair of rubber slippers. No trace of anyone else, such as a woman. No suggestive lace underwear hung up to dry, no glasses stained with lipstick, only the dust and moderate disorder of an old bachelor's place, and nothing else. His children and wife would always be left with this question. What did it mean, that rented room in a public housing estate in a city that was not his own? When did Papa go there? Why did he never tell us? The truth is that the room held no secrets. There was no mystery apart from what you could see: detective novels, a few cigarettes, a glass of grappa, a pad of charcoal sketches. A room for forgetting, every now and again, that he was a husband, a father, a precise, punctual worker, a man who could always be counted on, regardless. A room in which to be alone. As Virginia Woolf might define it: *A Room of One's Own*.

★

In the little village of Talamone, in Uccellina National Park in the province of Grosseto, lived an old retired fisherman. Early in the morning, in summer or winter, come rain or shine, he would get his fishing boat ready, have his dog board the boat, and set off fishing alone. I watched him go out to sea and return many times. Even during winter, the boat would slide slowly along the surface of the water like a blue-grey walnut shell in the pouring rain. From afar, the man was little more than a tiny silhouette against the light. I knew he would come home with his catch, hang his old hat on a nail by the door to his house, cook and sit outside on the veranda. He would turn two fruit crates upside down and stack them to make a little table, with the step in front of the door as a seat. The dog. The wine. The freshly caught fish. The silence. He was already well past the age when he expected anything in particular from life. Now he had had what he had, and his fate had been settled. There was no horizon to be reached at all costs. Instead he could look at the blue horizon that pushed as far as the islands: Giglio, Giannutri, Elba. No-one asked him too many questions. He was still capable of taking care of himself, of making his living like a real fisherman or subsistence hunter. He lived alone, but he was not isolated. He could go out in his boat and return when he was tired. No-one was waiting for him with a plate set on the table and anxiety stuck in their throat. A man who is alone is a free man.

★

The director Ingmar Bergman must also have felt this way, but a little village looking out onto the sea was not enough for him. He needed an island, so an island it was. His home from the sixties onwards was the island of Fårö, in the Baltic Sea, east of the Swedish coast. A flat, rocky, wind-battered island of which Bergman writes in his autobiography:

> This is your landscape, Bergman. It corresponds to your innermost imaginings of forms, proportions, colours, horizons, sounds, silences, lights and reflections. Security is here . . . a counterweight to the theatre. If I were to rant and rave on the shore, a gull, at most, would take off. On the stage, such an exhibition would be disastrous . . . I would retreat from the world, read the books I hadn't read, meditate, cleanse my soul . . . Self-imposed solitude is alright. I entrenched myself and established machine-like routines. I got up early, went for a walk, worked and read.[†]

After long months in theatres or on a film set, the island of Fårö gave Bergman a chance to unplug and plug in elsewhere, to fuel his creative machine from a different source. Solitude, managed well, can produce considerable energy.

*

†     Ingmar Bergman, *The Magic Lantern, an Autobiography*, trans. Joan Tate (London: Hamish Hamilton, 1988), 208–9.

But as Bergman writes, solitude is alright when it has been consciously chosen, less so when it is imposed on you from the outside, when you suddenly find that other people have abandoned you for whatever reason, or when you feel that you no longer have anything in common with them. This is the crucial difference between solitude and isolation.

It was 1972 and Leonardo Vitale had been locked up in Barcellona Pozza di Gotta, the psychiatric prison in Sicily. He was a little more than thirty years old. He had been arrested and charged with taking part in a kidnapping, and then released due to lack of proof. But after the arrest, something snapped inside him and he decided to tell someone his story. He presented himself to the judge and confessed to being part of a powerful criminal association: Cosa Nostra. It was hard to believe him, in those years when no-one spoke of the Mafia and superficially no-one knew anything. His allegations could not be proven and he was emotionally disturbed. He claimed to have been a "man of honour" or mafioso since 1960, affiliated with the Altarello di Baida family under his uncle's command, to have performed his first execution as a boy. After several breakdowns, he was committed to an institution, much to the Mafia's relief, since the allegations of a certified madman would have no legal value. He spent ten years in Barcellona Pozzo di Gotta, the psychiatric prison in the province of Messina, alone with his truth. His revelations would never be investigated. On 2 December, 1984, two months after being freed, he was shot as he stepped out of a church. It would be years before the most important state witnesses confirmed his accusations.

Rita was a Sicilian girl from Partanna in the province of Trapani. She was only eleven years old when her father, Don Vito, a shepherd by profession and a high-ranking mafioso, nicknamed "the peacemaker" for his skill in settling quarrels, was murdered before her eyes. She was sixteen on 24 June, 1991, when her brother Nicola, who belonged to a new generation of Mafia foot soldiers, was murdered as well. They had become very close after her father's death. For many years, Nicola had treated her not as his pampered youngest sister but as a confidante, someone with whom he could discuss his money matters, drug dealing, friendships, insults, the hierarchy. Rita was also close to Nicola's wife, Piera Aiello, who decided to turn state witness after her husband's death, to speak up, to reveal everything she knew. Rita was a girl, but she understood her sister-in-law. She was on her side, despite the fact that as a state witness, Piera would be sent to live far away under police protection. Now Rita was alone. She had no-one to turn to: her boyfriend had broken up with her because she was the sister-in-law of a *pentita*, a betrayer, and betrayal was an ugly, unforgivable thing. Even her mother, Giovanna, disapproved of Piera's decision and never wanted to hear her name mentioned again. Rita spent anguished days locked in her room writing in her diary. But she could not remain silent any longer, so in November of that year she decided to inform on the Mafia, to expose everything she knew about the organization in which she had lived since she was born. What began as revenge soon turned into something else. She realized that the Mafia was a cancer that had to be battled, beginning in people's hearts. That was how she met Paolo Borsellino, and began her life in hiding in Rome. It is hard to imagine the days this girl would spend holed up in an apartment in a city that was not hers, that she did not know. Of course she was with Piera now, but the hours must have seemed long when spent in the company of a notebook, pen and memories that offered no respite. When a car bomb on via d'Amelio in Palermo killed Magistrate Borsellino and his escort of five police officers on 19 July, 1992, Rita gave up: now she truly had no-one left. One week later, on July 26, she put an end to her life by throwing herself from the seventh floor of number 23 viale Amelia in Rome, where she had been living in hiding and protected as a state witness.

I could not help noticing the coincidence between the names of the street where the magistrate was killed and the street where Rita committed suicide. It struck me as though it had been designed by fate, even though one should not believe in fate. While turning the pages of this brave, proud girl's diary, I underlined in pencil the fear, the anguish and the sense of profound solitude, solitude of the harmful kind, which illuminated her words with an unhappy lunar light:

> *A subtle, dreary darkness pervades you,*
> *but this time it is not fear that is blocking your*

> *sight, it is the evening itself,*
> *it is the faint light of the moon that is slowly,*
> *slowly, sweetly, putting yours out*
> *until it has almost made you die inside.*

Rita Atria would be alone even in death, publicly repudiated by her mother, who destroyed the photo on the tombstone of her "spying, tattletale daughter" with a hammer.

Boxes of solitude, walls that tighten around you without escape, without an opening that might let a breath of fresh air in. You could easily die in one of those boxes. A few years ago, leafing through the pages of newspapers I had collected over the past couple of months, I noticed a curious assonance between three news stories that broke at roughly the same time, three dramatic and bizarre cases.

### MAN DIES OF SOLITUDE IN A BOX

A man in Monza disappeared for two months and no-one searched for him. He evidently had neither family nor any other particularly close ties. Then his neighbours began to notice a strange smell, and that was how they found him: by then he was a corpse locked up in a wooden chest in his garage. The article does not reveal the precise cause of death, which may have been a stroke or heart attack, definitely not a suicide. What we do know is that this man had designed and constructed a shelter bunker, of the kind children make, like a tree-house or a tepee put up in a bedroom. In it he had put a Walkman for listening to music, a screwdriver, a pair of glasses, water, croissants and a few cushions. A protected space, invented perhaps to play at survival, a place in which to return to being a child and to hide from even the most harmless scrutiny. A refuge that turned into a fatal trap.

The second news item was from Orenburg, Russia, in the Ural Mountains.

### WOMAN ORDERS HER FOUR CHILDREN TO DIE BY BEING BURIED ALIVE IN A STORAGE ROOM

In June 2003, a 36-year-old woman and her four children locked themselves in a tiny room used for storing rubbish bins (the woman worked as a rubbish collector and had no home), closing the door from the inside and destroying the keyhole with pliers. For two months, no-one searched for them. Finally, the plywood board affixed to the window fell and a terrible smell assailed the street. Five skeletons: one woman and four children, all dead of hunger and thirst. Then, the miracle: one of the children, the oldest, Dilovari, called Dima, aged thirteen – turned out to be alive. He was malnourished and dehydrated, nearly blind, but perhaps he would survive.

I keep asking myself what has become of that boy, whether he is alive and what his life is like now. And whether he will ever be able to understand and forgive his mother's act. Alone and desperate, she may have thought that the only way to protect her children would be to make them disappear. She had told them that their father had abandoned them and that no-one needed them any longer.

Two horrifying stories from two different worlds, I thought: a bored man, a desperate woman. Completely different stories, and yet their desperation may have had the same roots. This reminded me of the phenomenon of the so-called *hikikomori*, Japanese teenagers or young adults who never leave their rooms and only communicate with the outside world via the internet. The world is reduced to an L.C.D. screen that emanates a constant, moon-like glow, day and night, while these pale, sad figures are shut up in their rooms, earphones plugged in, their fingers tapping out words on a keyboard, words that will be sent into an unknown universe populated by other ethereal beings similar to themselves.

The third news item concerns seven young people below the age of twenty who were found dead in Tokyo inside a minivan parked in Nimoyama Park, the park of the Mountain of Beauty; according to the article, it was probably the result of a suicide pact planned online.

★

What kind of world is this, I thought, this world in which people decide to die in boxes of solitude? What is so terrible about the world outside? Why has the sky darkened?

A period of solitude can be one stage in a spiritual journey, like the Hindu initiation rite in which the participant leaps over a fire and runs away into the forest. He has to remain there for a certain period, looking within himself in order to learn to go beyond himself, before he can return to the community. Today we seldom think of a period of solitude, such as a long journey, as a formative experience. Who knows, perhaps the world has become too dangerous, too full of snares, and in any case there is no time to travel for the sole purpose of looking, knowing, putting yourself to the test. We travel the way we do everything else: almost always in a rush, almost always because we have to, distracted, but also extremely picky, incapable of accepting the basic rule of real travel: that it is unplanned and wasteful. A waste of money, of time, and above all, of one's self. Because serious travel involves throwing away preconceptions, the already seen and felt, giving up convenient prejudices and opening one's eyes, head and heart to the unknown, which includes what we carry inside us. Those who have never travelled alone are little acquainted with themselves: to be alone in an unfamiliar place among strangers whose language you do not speak is to put yourself to the ultimate test, to find out what you are made of. In my travels, I very rarely come across people who are travelling alone. Italians, in particular, almost always travel as couples or in groups, and regard solitary travellers with suspicion. Moreover, hardly anyone I know would go to the cinema or a restaurant alone. It is as though anything that is not shared does not exist or is less interesting. As though fear itself were always there, ready to snatch us away with its giant claws the moment we let go of the hand holding our own to cross the street. We thus continue to live with crutches – or "mobility aids", as today's politically correct language would have it.

Who knows, maybe we are neither healthy nor innocent, the prerequisites that Thoreau considered necessary for hearing a music that resonates even in the worst and most terrifying storms. We evidently have a growing fear of the solitude of Nature, of the undomesticated wild. It is no coincidence that the population of Italy's mountains has dwindled over the last few decades, leaving only old people in the beautiful villages of the Apennines and the Alps. Houses fall into disrepair and millennia-old traditions fade while the cities swell, growing visibly larger and fatter, in constant need of more space for their overweight cement sprawl. Everyone – or almost everyone – wants to be near the centre, wants the convenience of living within walking distance of the shops, cinema, a so-called social life. Everyone wants to be where the action is. But as Thoreau wrote, "What do we want most to dwell near to?" A wise man does not want to be near to the railway station, the post office, the school, ". . . but to the perennial source of our life . . ."

Does living amid a forest of buildings and thousands of other human beings allow us to feel near enough to the perennial source of our life?

I have lived all my life in Budrio, a village seventeen kilometres from Bologna. It is from Budrio that I left to explore the world, and to Budrio that I returned. The distance from the city never used to bother me, there was and is a small train (on the Bologna–Portomaggiore line which used to be called *La Veneta*) that covers the full distance in twenty-five minutes. Only evenings were and still are a problem, because the last train is at 9 p.m. The cinema is out of the question unless you drive. And driving through the foggy plains in winter can be unpleasant and put you off the idea. For the past two years, as a result of circumstance rather than choice, I have been living in the centre of Bologna, in a narrow street lined with many doors. It does not get more central than this: Piazza Maggiore is a five-minute walk away. When there is a political rally I can hear it from my balcony. But here in the city centre, I am more alone than I was in the countryside at Budrio. I had never lived in a block of flats and I would not have known, if I had not been told, that the closer together you live, the further you are from each other. The corridors in these buildings are often lonely places: people look furtive, suspicious, they smile half smiles that fade quickly. Keys in hand, they hurry to double-lock themselves behind reinforced doors into their apartments. In the flat we can hear the voices and sometimes the slightest movements of bodies on the other side of the wall; we get used to the daily schedule and goings-on of our next-door neighbours but know nothing more about them than what we might glean from an argument inadvertently overheard. In Budrio I lived in a flat carved out of the annex of an eighteenth-century villa surrounded by a large, Italian-style garden. There were seven flats arranged in an L shape, as well as the central villa and the park. We were all young tenants who held strange jobs. For a few years, our lives became magically and diabolically inter-twined. We loved and hated each other, consoled and irritated each other by turns, we celebrated weddings and baptisms, cooked together, and threw parties in the park. There was always someone rapping at the door or on the shutters someone who needed an egg, two hundred grams of flour, advice, a working computer, a condom. There were no rules or schedule; we all knew the most intimate details of each other's lives, and stayed up until two in the morning analysing each other's lives over dozens of bottles of wine generously provided by Mario the Philosopher, whose apartment was the common room. Some-times it drove me mad. I would lock the doors and windows, shut the cats up indoors and declare: I want to be alone, this is hell. They called me the "immured but alive" one. Although I enjoyed that way of living, I still needed space for solitude. The park was surrounded by a residential silence that I have always disliked. Suburban housing districts have spread like an oil stain over the last few years, segregated communities sold as "paradises of tranquillity", terraced houses that resemble maximum-security prisons more than they do real homes, with their solid doors, bars at every window and railings in front of doors, and alarm systems, devised and built to discourage taking a breath of fresh air. The outside world is nothing but danger anyway. In their cars, in sealed compartments with air conditioning, people travel from home to work, from work to a shopping mall, and then back home. They each have their own little square of garden, their garage, basement, the sacrosanct right to their own private piece of the world. Their rightful slice of solitude. Where a community should exist, there is nothing left. Suburban silence is interrupted by the barking of dogs, the howling of alarms set off by a gust of wind, and the hum of televisions left switched on. The hell of suburban solitude.

I was recently struck by a newspaper ad: Andy Garcia, the American actor with a tough guy's face and tender heart, looking out from between two massive doors: "When it comes to my private space, I won't allow intrusion." In another version of the same ad, Garcia, wearing a mysterious, unsmiling expression, leans on the steel frame of a window that looks as though it could be in a maximum-security prison: "When I am acting / I close my windows to the world and no-one / can get in." The logo is followed by the firm's motto: "your home, your life." It is our home and our life, but is this really what we want? Reinforced doors and windows designed to shut the world out? If that is the case, where is the crack? Clearly there must be a crack, a rift, in a system of values that exalts isolation and total security as a model lifestyle, and then decries solitude as an absolute social ill.

In conclusion, the question is: when are you alone? And what does it mean to be alone? Not having a wife, a boyfriend, a lover? Not having a family, or friends? Or not being close, as Thoreau would put it, to the "perennial source of our life"? Perhaps there exists a different answer for every person. To me, being alone is a normal condition; whether I have or don't have company, family, or friends is beside the point. It has allowed me to learn a lot about myself and about the world. Being alone lets you open up to the unknown. It lets you discover that the world does not have to be a hostile place in which we must guard ourselves against anyone outside the restricted circle of people we know and trust. We find that solitudes can meet. And that solitude, unlike its evil cousin, isolation, can be an extraordinary way of exercising freedom.

TRANSLATED BY CHENXIN JIANG

PIERO COLAPRICO (Putignano, 1957) is the author of crime novels including *La Trilogia della città di M.* (1994, winner of Premio Scerbanenco), and of a series co-written with Pietro Valpreda featuring Maresciallo Binda, which he has continued to write alone since Valpreda's death. He has been a special correspondent for *La Repubblica* since 1985, covering crime-related issues, and coined the term "Tangentopoli", referring to a system of bribery and corruption in Milan, a few months before the Pio Albergo Trivulzio scandal broke. His book on the subject, *Capire Tangentopoli* (1996), is one of several published works of high-profile journalism.

CARLO LUCARELLI (Parma, 1960) is a crime writer, television presenter and magazine editor. His first crime novels formed the Commissario de Luca Trilogy, and were followed by the Ispettore Grazia Negro mysteries, of which *Almost Blue* was shortlisted for the C.W.A. Gold Dagger in 2003. He has written screenplays and radio plays, and is a singer in the post-punk band Progetto K. He was co-founder together with Marcello Fois and Loriano Machiavelli of "Gruppo 13", a writers' collective in the Emilia-Romagna area, and teaches at Alessandro Baricco's Holden School in Turin, as well as at Padova's maximum-security prison.

VALERIA PARRELLA (Naples, 1974) is an actor for the theatre and a short story writer. For her volume *Mosca più balena* she was awarded the Premio Campiello in 2004. Her subsequent collection *Per grazia ricevuta* (2004, published in English as *For Grace Received* in 2009) was shortlisted for the Premio Strega, the Premio Renato Fucini and the Premio Zerilli-Marimò. Her most recent book, *Antigone*, was published by Einaudi Editore in 2012.

ROBERTO SAVIANO (Naples, 1979) writes for *La Repubblica* and *L'Espresso*, as well as for many newspapers around the world. After the publication of *Gomorrah* (now translated into forty languages) and its subsequent film adaptation (winner of the Grand Prix at Cannes in 2008) he received several death threats, obliging the Italian government to provide him with 24-hour protection. He has been living in hiding since 2006. In 2011 he was awarded the PEN/Pinter Prize, and in that year his collection of essays, *Beauty and the Inferno* (MacLehose Press) appeared in English translation.

SIMONA VINCI (Milan, 1970) was awarded the Premio Elsa Morante for her first novel *Dei bambini non si sa niente* (1999), controversial for its depiction of sexuality amongst a group of younger and older children. A bestseller in Italy and translated into twelve languages, it was published in English as *A Game We Play* to enormous critical acclaim.

THE WU MING FOUNDATION describes itself as "a mysterious collective of guerrilla novelists from Italy". The writers' collective was formed in 2000 out of the Luther Blissett Project, an existing group of hundreds of artists and social activists across Europe. "Wu-Ming" is Chinese for "anonymous" or "five names", depending on how you pronounce the first syllable, and is a byline among Chinese citizens demanding democracy and freedom of speech. Together they are the authors of more than fifteen novels, of which *Q*, *54* and *Manituana* are available in English.

# Camilleri, Lucarelli and De Cataldo

## JUDGES

*Translated from the Italian by Joseph Farrell, Alan Thawley and Eileen Horne*

Camilleri, best known for his Inspector Montalbano series, presents the charming **Judge Surra** who moves to a small Sicilian town in the late nineteenth century. He does not quite understand the quirky welcoming gifts from the locals, but nothing stands in the way of his quest for justice – and pastries.

Lucarelli brings us a far darker story. Judge Valentina Lorenzi – **La Bambina** – is so young and inexperienced she hardly merits a bodyguard. But when she barely survives an assassin's bullet, her black-and-white world of crime and punishment turns a deathly shade of grey.

In **The Triple Dream of the Prosecutor**, De Cataldo, a judge himself, crafts a Kafkaesque tale of a lifelong feud between Prosecutor Mandati and the corrupt Mayor of Novere. When the mayor narrowly escapes a series of bizarre assassination attempts, Mandati begins to realise that all his dreams may just be coming true.

## MACLEHOSE PRESS

www.maclehosepress.com

*Subscribe to our quarterly newsletter*